TRESPASS

By LaVina Vanorny-Barcus

TRESPASS

By LaVina Vanorny-Barcus

Chapter #1

Always erase the call and texting history on your phone…

"GET OUT!!" She yelled at him, her face livid with anger and frustration. Her hands were clenched so tightly that her nails dug into her palms. The tears rolled down her cheeks making discolored streaks in her makeup as they flowed down her face. "I want you out of here NOW!!"

"But Betsy!" he pleaded with his blue eyes and dark lashes. "I can explain! It's not what you think!"

"Oh really?" she said mockingly pretending to talk like him. "Please come to my house on Friday. My wife is out of town so you can spend the night." She sniffed loudly. She was a woman who should never cry. Her nose ran like a sieve and her eyes were rimmed bright pink.

She started to shout again with her voice raising an octave even higher than before. "That text message speaks for itself! No explanation needed! Get out!"

He walked toward her with his arms stretched out on each side, with a big smile on his face. He thought maybe if he put his arm around her she would listen to what he had to say. She shoved his outstretched arm out of the way roughly with both hands. He instinctively pushed back. She lost her balance and fell back against the table scraping her arm on the wooden edge as she fell.

"Get out of my house NOW!" She grabbed his cell phone off of the table where she had been reading it and threw it at the front door with all of the force she could muster. The back cover flew off as the phone cracked the glass window in the door. The cover and the phone landed on the tile floor with loud claps. He could see the screen of his phone was shattered like a meticulously woven spider web.

Realizing he needed to let her cool off, he hastily bent down and gathered up the parts of his phone and headed out the door slamming it shut behind him in defiance. A large chard of glass slipped from the broken door's window frame and shattered into thousands of pieces on the cement front step causing a glitter of broken glass, sparkling in the halo from the porch light.

Even with all that, he wasn't worried. She always cooled down and she always backed down. She had let him come back home in the past and within a few days their relationship would be good again. He was sure of it.

Peter Johnson always pushed the limits when it came to cheating. The last time he was caught, his wife saw him out for dinner with a young lady when he was supposed to be out of town visiting his mother. But he explained and pleaded that he had accidently bumped her car in the parking lot and took her out to eat in order to keep them from getting sued. See…he always had *their* best interest at heart.

He flashed that flirty smile that women rarely could resist as he thought of that girl. God was she pretty! After Betsy threw a big fit in front of her at the restaurant she refused to accept his phone calls. What a shame. He would have liked to get to know her better. Another missed opportunity.

Peter was twenty nine years old and was a full six foot four inches tall. He had blonde highlights and thought of himself as a lady's man. He had been very popular on his college campus. He had been the president of his Fraternity and enjoyed the prestige and the impressive power it gave him.

He met Betsy Jacobs at a fraternity party after the University homecoming football game. He was leaning against the front door frame drinking a red solo cup full of beer and suddenly he froze when he saw her from across the room.

Betsy was very striking with long blonde hair, golden and silky. Her brown eyes were deep and animated as she conversed with a male friend. She had a tall slender body, muscular from years of aerobics and healthy eating. He found out that she was also very committed to her college studies. Her ambition was to become a Certified Public Accountant. He went over to talk to her immediately and worked his way in between she and the guy she was speaking with. Soon he had her full attention and asked her out for dinner.

She replied, "No, I'm sorry. I appreciate the offer but I really need to study. I have several exams next week and I want to do well."

He wasn't used to being dismissed by a female. Over the next few weeks he asked her out three more times with the same results until the fourth time when she finally agreed to go out with him. His interest was piqued and his ego needed some strokes to the point that he became obsessed with her and spent most of his senior year trying to impress her. Bouquets of flowers, boxes of luscious chocolates and expensive bottles of wine were delivered weekly, sometimes even more often. Whatever it would take…that was his motto.

After graduation Betsy accepted an accounting internship several states away to provide her with experience while she studied for her CPA exams. He did not want to lose her, not to a job or to anyone, so in desperation he asked her to marry him and she surprised him by saying 'yes'.

Peter, despite his outward apparent confidence, was really insecure inside. He feared she would change her mind so he developed an elaborate plan to 'kidnap' her and head to Las Vegas. Betsy was so flattered she went along with the whirlwind plan and at a small chapel, officiated by Elvis, they both declared "I do."

After they were married things were great, but she still had to study for her CPA exams, day after day, night after night. Peter started to get bored being married to a student, until he met Jenny.

Peter had received a degree in Liberal Arts and was hired at the local post office. Civil Service jobs paid well and allowed Peter a lot of benefits including the hope of a large retirement fund. He felt very lucky to have landed a federal job.

Jenny was a mail carrier that he saw every morning when she loaded her mail truck with the day's receipts.   She wasn't as beautiful as Betsy but she had a flirty personality that he found very attractive. He especially liked her green eyes. He made sure to *coincidently* be around the loading dock whenever she pulled up.

"Hey gorgeous!" He flirted with her, displaying a big smile on his face, as he looked intensely into her green eyes. "Do you need help with your truck today?"

"That would be great!" She answered with enthusiasm as she carried a stack of boxes, all wrapped in tape and brown paper, from the back door of the post office to the back of her truck. "I'm trying to get done early tonight."

"Well, if you are going to get off early tonight how about we get together for a few drinks?" Peter asked confidently, flashing that huge smile that rarely ever missed. "How about going to Joe's Tap at the end of the block?"

"Oh, I'm sorry," Jenny said apologizing, obviously taken off guard. "But I wanted off early because I have a date with my boyfriend and I want to change clothes before he comes." She started to play with the end of her long auburn pony tail nervously.

Peter froze. *"Boyfriend?"* He asked confused, "I didn't know you had a *boyfriend.*"

"Oh sure," She said matter of fact. We have been going out for several months now." She stopped and looked bewildered. "Is that a problem?"   She could tell from his fast change of demeanor that it was.

"Well, I thought we had a connection." Peter spat at her angrily. "You should have told me!"   He threw her bag of mail into the back of her truck with more force than necessary and it flipped over top side down, spilling letters onto the metal floor. He turned heel and stomped back into the main office of the building without another word.

He slipped his phone out of his pocket and text her, 'You used me.' She never replied back.

Later that day a note was laying on his desk that simply said 'Peter' on the front.

Peter,

I'm so sorry you misunderstood my friendliness. My boyfriend is very generous to me and I am very devoted to him. I thought you were just being a nice guy. I had no idea you were interested in a romantic relationship. Hopefully we can still be friends.
Jenny

As Peter read the note, his boss walked into his office.   Peter quickly shoved the envelope into his denim coat pocket. His boss was very strict about his employee's work ethic and would not appreciate him spending time on personal matters, especially with another employee.

He forgot about the note in his coat pocket until Betsy threw it at him the next day when he got home from work. She angrily accused him of wanting to have an affair. But she accepted his explanation just like she did so many times over the years.

Chapter #2

Make sure to have your finances in order.

Sergeant Williams hated making this kind of call. Restraining orders and divorces were such annoying work. He couldn't sympathize with either party as he had to remain neutral as part of his job. But sometimes he felt things were not very balanced for one party or the other.

This current restraining order was issued as preventative and he knew domestic situations could sometimes escalate quickly. It was very necessary to make sure some distance was maintained to give both parties a chance to cool off.

He entered the door to the post office and stood in line behind a heavy set lady buying stamps who was complaining about how much they cost.

"I can't believe you can sleep at night with the amount you charge to mail such a light weight letter! And another thing…" When she realized a police officer was standing behind her she stopped mid sentence and gathered up her things and left quickly. He thought it was amusing how people reacted when they saw him wearing his uniform, conducting official business. Most people avoided looking him in the eye and usually they went out of their way to get out of his way.

Sergeant Williams was a police detective but in a lot of smaller towns all officers chipped in to help do these routine duties. Today, it was his turn.

The HR department at the main post office had been very helpful. They informed him that a Peter Johnson worked at the downtown mail sorting office. And that was the purpose for his visit today.

The clerk at the counter looked nervous as she politely asked, "May I help you...Sir?" Her cheeks flushed as she paused.

"Hello." The Sergeant flipped out his detective badge for the clerk to see. He was a big man who looked even bigger with his bullet proof vest underneath his heavily starched uniform shirt. He had just turned fifty but felt he still had some good years left in him. His hair was graying but he was lucky to have a thick head full. He always kept himself clean shaven, though once in a while he let himself grow stubble on the weekends simply out of laziness and because he could.

"Would a Peter Johnson be available for me to speak with?" The Sergeant consulted his paperwork as he spoke to ensure he had the correct name. The anxious clerk picked up the phone to make a call. "Just a moment, please."

The phone was picked up in one ring. "Hello?"

"Mr. Posia? There is a police detective here to see Peter. Could you come and escort him for me? I'm alone at the desk and can't leave." The clerk kept fidgeting and looked up at the Sergeant nervously.

"I'll be right out."

"That is our boss, Mr. Jerry Posia." She said as she put the phone back in its cradle. "He will be right with you, Officer."

"Thank you for your help." The officer walked over to a bulletin board to read as he waited. The crumbling cork board was filled with flyers from upcoming neighborhood events and pictures of the new stamps that you could order. Many of them were aimed at wedding invitations since they were pictures of big white roses and curls of ribbons, sometimes circling the word "Love."

The big double metal door squeaked open behind the officer and Jerry Posia hurried into the lobby.

"Jerry Posia," he said with his hand extended to the officer.

"I'm Sergeant Williams.   I'm here to serve some papers to a Peter Johnson. Is he available?" He said as he quickly shook the man's hand.

"Yes," said Jerry. "I'll take you to him. Just follow me."

"Thank you for your help." And he stepped in line behind the stocky man.

"He's in our back office working on mail holds. But you can talk to him as long as you need to."

"Can I ask what mail holds are?" asked the officer out of sheer curiosity.

"When our customers go out of town for business or vacation they can elect to have us hold their mail instead of stuffing it in their mail box, day after day." Jerry spoke as he continued to lead the way to the back of the large room.

"Then when people return home, they can come down to our office and get their mail. People do it mainly for safety and convenience."

"Sounds like a wise idea," agreed the Sergeant, nodding in approval.

By now they could see Peter back in an office area, working away, sorting mail that would be held for customers that had requested it. It was a very manual process and was one of Peter's varied responsibilities.

"Peter?" asked Jerry quietly and apologetically. "This is Sergeant Williams. He needs to speak to you."

The salt and pepper haired police officer filled the entire doorway of the office. His air of authority, his uniform plus his muscular physique, conveyed he held a position of power.

"Excuse me. Are you Peter Johnson?"

"Yes I am." Peter said cautiously, his heart started to beat rapidly. "Can I help you?"

The officer pulled a large manila envelope out from inside a black leather folder and dropped it onto Peter's desk.

"You have been legally served." The officer turned and walked out of the door with no change of expression and no further explanation.

"What the…" Peter said out loud. He tore open the stiff envelope and pulled out the papers. "A restraining order?? You have got to be kidding me!!"

"Having a tough day?" asked his boss from the doorway. "Did I hear you say *restraining order*?" Jerry walked in and helped himself to one of the green cloth chairs sitting in front of the old worn desk.

Peter's boss was a man named Jerry Posia. He was short in stature but very muscular and powerful looking. He had a short chunk of mustache that looked snarly beneath his nose. His dark wavy hair was unruly but that helped hide the growing bald spot on the back of his head.

"Yes," Peter spat out. "She says I assaulted her this morning. She fell against the table and

I guess she scraped her arm. But it wasn't my fault. I didn't do anything!"

He crumbled the paper up in his fist and threw it into the metal trash can by his desk, as if that might make it go away.

"It never is...but it *always* is." Jerry shook his head knowingly. "That's why I'm no longer married and have no plans to remarry."

"What if I run into her at the grocery store? Am I supposed to leave my groceries in the middle of the aisle and run out the door?" Peter said sarcastically still thinking about the document.

"It's not something you should mess around with," answered Jerry in a matter of fact voice. "I would do whatever you have to do to follow what it says. You can get in a lot of trouble if not." Jerry reached into the trash can and retrieved the wadded up document. He carefully opened it up and laid it on the desk, smoothing it out with his hands.

"I guess I can't go home tonight. But how are we supposed to work this out if I can't even call or text her?" Peter asked with desperation in his voice, "This is ridiculous!"

"Good luck." Jerry muttered while getting up to leave the room. He shook his head and added simply, "Been there, done that."

Peter decided that staying at a local hotel would be the best idea for tonight. He walked into the lobby of The Chateau through its massive rotating door, constructed out of glass and sparkling brass. The lobby was impressive with its white marble tiled floors and dark intricate woodwork.

The clerk behind the desk was dressed sharply, creased pants and a navy blue brocade vest with a gold colored tie. He was a middle aged man but had apparently had been at his job for many years. You could tell he appreciated his customers by the way he addressed Peter.

"May I help you, Sir?" He asked Peter, giving him his full attention.

"Yes, I would like a room for the night."

"King size or Queen?" The clerk said as he searched his computer for vacancies.

"Queen is fine."

"And how will you pay?"

"I'll use my debit card," replied Peter as he pulled it out of his billfold and handed it over to the robotic acting man, who obviously did this same routine successfully dozens of times each day.

Peter stood leaning against the polished wood of the counter and watched as the man swiped his card. He noticed the man started to frown and was told, "It didn't go through. Let me try it again." And in response, he slid the card through the magnetic reader and punched in the amount for a second time.

"I'm sorry," Said the now officious man, handing the card back to Peter. "How do you want to pay?"

"What?" said Peter feeling the anger cursing through his body, "There is plenty of money in my account. Try it again."

"I'm sorry," said the man, matter of fact. "Our policy is to only run cards twice or sometimes we'd be here all night trying."

Peter hastily opened his thin billfold and saw that he only had fifty dollars left in cash because he usually relied on his debit card. Unfortunately his credit card was still at his house. He knew that a room at this hotel would cost three times the piddle amount he carried on him.

"Sorry to have bothered you," Peter said with disdain, completely humiliated. He stumbled out of the lobby as fast as he could, by pushing the rotating door harder than it was programmed to move. He vowed that he would never walk into that hotel again.

He decided an inexpensive motel, located down the street, was his best option for tonight until the bank opened the next day. He was checking in at the beat up old front desk just as police were raiding a room on the ground floor searching for drugs. He watched while a straggly looking guy, whose pants drooped down low on his hips exposing his tattered skivvies, and a very skinny girl, whose hair probably hadn't been combed for a week, were led out of the first floor room to a waiting police car in hand cuffs. The guy was yelling obscenities and stumbling over his own feet the whole way. The girl was crying hysterically, sobbing like a two year old who missed her afternoon nap.

"Do you want the room by the hour or by the night?" The old man behind the counter asked bluntly, obviously oblivious to the police action occurring outside his check in window. He actually hummed a country western tune and smiled as he typed away on the outdated computer.

"Ah…by the night," said Peter hesitantly, surprised at the question.

"A big spender then," mused the hotel desk clerk. "How will you pay?"

"Cash," Peter said. He definitely didn't want to be humiliated in a place like this in case his debit card was rejected. In the end it took almost all of his cash to stay there for the 'whole' night. He needed to visit the bank first thing the next morning.

Finally Peter headed outside, through the wet windy weather, to door 3A. The rusty hinges screeched open after using the faded scratched up card to unlock the door. He held the card by the tippy corner as if germs would crawl up his arm if he touched it more than that.

Peter didn't have any luggage since all of his clothes were still at his house. He'd have to go to the police station tomorrow to see what he would need to do to get access to them.

The room had obviously been a smoking room for a long time. I think we are talking a smoking room for years, many years! The stale odor hit Peter like a greasy fry pan in his face as soon as he opened the door. The smell was ingrained strongly in every fiber that existed in the room.

He removed his boxers and T shirt and put them into the bathroom tub to try to wash them with the provided bar soap. Luckily he wore a uniform so no one would know it was going to be worn a second day in a row, except for the smoke smell.

The bed was lumpy and looked like it had not been changed from the last customer, or customers, so he decided to sleep on top of the comforter and use a blanket kept in the closet to keep warm.

Note to self: Get blankets from my house.

Peter had a fitful night of sleep. The walls were very thin and Peter could hear the amorous activities of the couple next door. He tried banging on the wall with his shoe to get them to quiet down but they just banged back, laughing loudly like it was some hilarious game.

His allergy problems were raising their ugly head, probably from the dust and smoky smell. After a few short hours he felt like his head would explode, it was so congested. And blowing his nose produced even more sinus pain, plus the room did not provide tissues so he had to use cheap toilet paper, scratchy and so thin it was almost transparent.

When he went to clean up the next morning he stepped into the shower and pulled the plastic curtain shut only to find a cockroach clinging to the mildewed fabric. It was waving its antennae around as if it was annoyed by the intrusion. Peter stepped right out and decided he didn't care to share his shower with something that carried more disease than the scum on the side of the tub did.

That morning he made it to work on time, but his pants and shirt were very wrinkly since the room did not come with hangers. Jerry smiled when he saw him walk in. "Looks like you slept in those clothes."

"Can you believe the roach motel down the street doesn't have an iron?"   Peter said laughing, but then ended up coughing from the congestion and sinus drainage.

"Sounds like you tied one on last night. I hope you'll still be able to work today. We have a busy one ahead of us."

Peter nodded his head since he was coughing too much to answer at that moment. He searched his coat pocket for a wadded up piece of toilet tissue and held it to his mouth, then unfolded it to blow his sore red nose.

Jerry just shook his head smiling that knowing smile.

"You'll need to talk to the police today so you can get your clothes. Stay away from the brown bottle flu and everything will get better," he said nodding his head and speaking from his own experience. Peter started to explain he hadn't been drinking but decided it didn't really matter, and he got busy processing a bin full of mail, though every time he bent down to reach inside, his throbbing head made him regret it.

Peter went to the police station on his lunch break, with all of his paperwork and was told a police escort would meet him at his house later that day.   They would call him with a scheduled time after finding out what would be *convenient* for Betsy.

"Here's a number for you to call if you have any questions about going into *her* home today." The female officer behind the desk stated.

Peter numbly took the paper.   The officer emphasized '*her home*' and Peter knew there was nothing he could do about it. He was just going to have to deal with it for now.

The bank teller was even less helpful. Betsy had cleaned out the bank account and because of the restraining order holds were placed on all of their savings, debit and credit cards. Peter no longer had access to any of their money. He tried to open a new account in his name only but the bank required an initial deposit of one hundred dollars before they would activate it. Unfortunately, he didn't have that much cash. He realized he would have to wait until he received his next paycheck. It looked like he would have no choice but to borrow some money to stay at the crummy roach motel for several more nights until he would have enough money to upgrade.

When he met the police officer later that afternoon he quickly went into his closet to gather his clothes. It felt so weird to be in the house, almost like he had never lived there.

He slid the closet door open and stood with his jaw hanging down to his chest. The closet was empty! His clothes were gone!! All of them! Including his work uniforms! He showed the police officer and the officer said it was a shame, but there was nothing he could do about it at this time.

The officer said routinely, "You'll need to get a lawyer."   He yawned and rubbed the stubble on his chin.

Chapter #3

Get your vehicles in both names

"Peter," said Jerry apologetically. "Sergeant Williams is here to speak with you. He has some more papers for you."

"More?" Questioned Peter obviously annoyed. The weight of the last two days showed plainly on his face and in his brightly rimmed red eyes.

The Sergeant held out two large envelopes. As Peter took them the Sergeant said, "You have been legally served. But I've been instructed to explain one of them."

"What is this about?" Peter questioned as he opened the first envelope. He read the first few lines and he quickly understood what it was about. "Divorce? She's filing for divorce?"

"There is a second letter. I suggest you should read that one now as well," stated Sergeant Williams flatly, ready to be done with this duty and off for the day.

Peter opened the envelope and started to read it. "Theft?" Peter exclaimed in disbelief. "She says I stole her car?"

"What car are you driving," asked the officer, who was totally void of emotion.

"A Lexus…why?"

"Is the registration in your name? Or in your wife's name?" asked Sergeant Williams even though he obviously already knew the answer to that.

"I'm not sure," said Peter looking upward with an eye roll as he tried to think. "I guess it's in her name. What difference does it make?"

"She wants it back." The officer stated flatly as he checked his paperwork. You get the 1998 Chevy Impala. If you will peacefully exchange cars with her she will withdraw the theft charges."

"Are you kidding me?" Argued Peter totally outraged. The sudden outburst of words clung in his throat and he started to cough again, very dry raspy coughs.

"No, she gets it if it's registered in her name only." Then he added, "You are just lucky that the Impala is in your name or you wouldn't have a car at all. Unless, of course, the divorce grants you one but that could be months down the road." Sergeant Williams checked the info on his clipboard as he spoke.

"You'll need to get yourself a lawyer."

The officer explained that the exchange would be made right now. A friend of Betsy's was outside with the Impala. Peter would get ten minutes to clear his things out of the Lexus.

"This doesn't seem fair!" Peter was turning red and the vein on the side of his head was throbbing. "It's not fair at all!"

"You shouldn't have assaulted her then," said the officer with as much emotion as if he was commenting on the weather. "Get the keys and let's go. She's waiting."

Peter quickly looked through the car to see what things he needed. He took his GPS and he had two garbage bags containing a blanket, a sheet set and a bed pillow. Other than his bathroom supplies that was about all he was able to take from his house the day before. He watched as his Lexus, which Betsy had purchased for him for his birthday, drove away and cruised around the corner until out of sight. He walked over to the old Impala. He loaded his things inside of the car and then saw an envelope sitting on the dash board.

"What now!" He thought. Opening envelopes had not been a pleasant activity lately.

Inside the envelope was a listing of all of their bills. A lawyer had neatly divided it in half showing what he would be responsible for until the divorce was final. He was to deliver the check monthly to the lawyer's office and they would make sure all of their bills were paid. He had no money or access to his savings. All of their credit cards were put on hold until the divorce was final. Between having to buy all new clothes, including uniforms and this bill, his entire monthly paycheck would be gone.

Peter guessed he would be sleeping at the cheap roach motel for at least a few more weeks.

Chapter #4

If plan A doesn't work, resort to plan B

Jerry sympathized with Peter. He told him he could use the office bathroom to get dressed in the morning if that would help. The post office building was very old and still had a shower stall with hot water that used to be provided for postal truck drivers in the old days of postal delivery.

Jerry brought Peter the paperwork in order to change his direct deposited paycheck to a new bank account. Peter filled it out feeling grateful for the help from Jerry. Peter would not receive a paycheck until that coming Friday so Jerry kindly lent him three hundred dollars to go buy some sweat pants and T shirts to wear when not at work. Socks and boxers were purchased too. This covered the one hundred needed to open the account plus it would cover a night or two in the hotel.

His money stretched pretty far since he shopped at a local discount store where things were cheap, though unfortunately they were also cheaply made. He couldn't be too choosy now. He just needed to get by. And he had a new plan for sleeping at night since he had very little money to spare, especially to be spent to sleep with roaches, drug addicts and smoke.

Peter ordered a new uniform, so he wouldn't have to wash his uniform every single night. It worked out great that he wouldn't get the bill until after Friday, payday. His entertainment for the night was sitting at the Laundromat washing his clothes. Pretty darn exciting.

Finally his clothes were dry and this time most of the wrinkles were out. It was time to head to his car. He decided to park in the post office parking lot, back behind the building, where the trucks load at the docks. He got his blanket and pillow and curled up in the back seat exhausted. The impala had a wider seat than the Lexus so maybe it wasn't too bad of a trade after all. Even though he wasn't all that comfortable, sleep came easily and soundly. Not too bad for a free night's stay.

"Hey you!" A gruff voice yelled. The man took his flashlight and tapped it against the car window repeatedly. "Wake up!"

Peter's eyes flew open and he tried to free himself from the tangle of blankets he was wrapped in. He tried to peer through the fog on the window but had to wipe the condensation off of the glass to see the police officer looking back in at him. He could see the police car lights swirling in the background and he started to panic. He frantically pushed the button to open the back window but he realized it wouldn't work until he started his car. He had to crawl over the front seat to get behind the wheel before he could start the car and open the window. He knew he looked ridiculous.

"Yes Officer?" he said with a dry croaking voice when he finally got the window down. "Can I help you?"

"Why are you sleeping in your car?" The officer demanded gruffly. "You cannot sleep in a government parking lot at night."

"I'm sorry," said Peter frustrated. "I got served with divorce papers and I work at the post office. I didn't know there was a law against myself being here. Where can I go?"

"Your home would be my first suggestion," said the officer. "Either way, it can't be here. I will be back and I need to find you gone or there will be charges." He turned heel and walked back to his car lit up like a Ferris wheel. The officer started his car with a roar and drove forward continuing his snake like inspection cruise through the parking lot and frontage road.

Peter felt like the whole world was against him. He put the Impala into drive and went to find somewhere that he could park for the night. He drove around for about a half hour until he saw the grocery store. It was open 24 hours per day so no one hopefully would notice him in the back of the lot or have a problem with it. The parking lot lights were so terribly bright that he had to pull the covers over his head. At least he managed a few hours of sleep.

In the morning he woke up to his cell phone alarm, sore and stiff. He drove to the post office to shower and dress for his day at work. Luckily the coffee pot was always on for the employees, and today he would need more than one cup.

"Glad to see you made it in Peter." Peter turned around to see Jerry standing there smiling. Jerry's cup of coffee had a full head of steam rising above it.

"Yup, I'm here. But I hope you have a lot of strong coffee. I think I'll need some!" Peter rubbed his eyes as he spoke. He knew he looked like death warmed over a couple of times. He felt like he had dragged his body to work that day and it had fought him every inch of the way. He had misplaced his razor so his stubble was noticeable, especially under his nose.

"Did you know you can't sleep in a government parking lot?" Jerry said laughing, holding his hand cupped over his mouth sheepishly.

"How did you know?"

"The police called me and reported someone homeless sleeping in the lot." Jerry smiled. "I kind of thought it might be you."

"Yeah, it was me." Peter said wishing no one had known what happened. He headed to the back of the office to start working on the mail holds for the day.

Just his luck.

Chapter #5

Photos are a good insurance policy

"5410 Sunset Road, Two weeks". Peter shook his head. "7310 Arrowhead Lane, One week."

Life really was unfair. These addresses were some of the ritziest zip codes in town. Not only did they live in amazing homes they also went on long vacations that were probably fabulous! So unfair!

"1723 Stoney Point, two weeks." This house wasn't in the very best neighborhood but it wasn't bad. In fact it was only two blocks down the street from the post office. Peter always thought it would be nice to live close to work. Sometimes the rush hour traffic was miserable and the hassle made him feel like he had worked half of a day just to get there!

He got a piece of scratch paper out of the drawer and wrote down the three addresses. Maybe he would drive by later, just for something to do. Without spending money his entertainment choices were pretty limited.

"Hey there," said a female voice casually behind him.

Peter turned around to find Jenny standing there with a smug smile on her face. He quickly folded and tucked the paper with the addresses on it in his shirt pocket, feeling immediately like the cat that swallowed the canary.

"Oh hi," Peter replied nervously. "Is your truck ready?"

"Yes," she replied cocking her head to one side in a playful way. Her auburn long hair was so silky and the color complimented her porcelain fair skin. "I got it loaded and I'm just in here checking to see if I missed anything."

"Well, none of your mail will be back here. I'm sure we had it all bagged." He dismissed her without another word and walked past her to the sorting area. *How dare she rub it in his face by coming back here to see him!* There was no other reason for her to come back there except to mock him. How dare her!

The rest of the day went by without any more deliveries from the police department or more annoying visits from Jenny. Thank goodness. He got caught up on his work and was prepared to sleep in his car again, under the bright lights of the super market parking lot but first he wanted to check out the houses on his hold list. He touched his pocket to make sure the list was still there.

Peter drove to the first house on the list. The home was massive, large stone façade, three fire places according to the chimneys, and a six car garage. In the window he saw a sticker stating the house was covered by a security system.

Peter drove up to the second house and saw a sparkling swimming pool in the back yard with a tennis court. It was three stories high and had a walkout back patio.   He wondered what kind of jobs people had that could afford homes like these. Or were the people just neck deep in debt? He pulled into the driveway and immediately many front lights turned on. Motion detectors. Again the security system stickers were in every window.

Peter then drove by the third house that was located on Stoney Point, which was an older part of town that *used* to be the ritzy area in its day. It was very well kept with a carefully manicured lawn and fresh paint. The house itself was probably built in the seventies. It reminded him of the house he grew up in, a story and a half. Except this house was updated with expensive stone and shutters and a beautiful patio had been added in back complete with a built in grill and hot tub.

It was quite dark outside now. All of the windows in the house were void of any lights or activity. Tall mature trees lined three sides of the house with thick foliage. No motion detecting lights turned on as he drove past. He turned down a desolate side street with no illuminating street lights and put his car into park.

He sat there for a few moments contemplating his next move. Would he really have the guts to be so bold?

He got out of his car making sure there weren't any 'no parking' signs posted along the street. Opening his car door sounded as loud as a radio blaring as it creaked open in the silence. He walked down the street trying to look nonchalant. But the more he concentrated on his movements the less natural they looked. He strode back toward the vacant house with his pillow, sheets and blanket wrapped up tightly like a back pack. He kept scanning the area to make sure no one was paying attention to him but luckily everyone was inside doing their regular evening routines. No one watched as he skirted the dark trees and shadows on the edge of the property. No one watched as he quietly slipped behind the house and stayed concealed in the darkness as he approached the back service door to the garage.

And hopefully, no one watched as he tested the metal service door, to find out that it was not locked. He stepped inside and closed the door behind him quietly. The garage was empty, except for a few shelves full of motor oil containers and bug spray. A tool holder adorned one wall, complete with a snow shovel and a hoe. It smelled damp and musty but looked very clean and completely organized.

He walked stealthily up to the door that led into the house and was disappointed when the knob stayed stationery and was locked. He pulled a credit card out of his billfold to try to unlock it by sliding it in between the door and the frame. The credit card started to shred on one side but it didn't matter since the account had been frozen, making it basically worthless.

As he slid it downward it refused to budge. He grasped it with both hands and jerked it downward as hard as he could. A loud click told him he had succeeded! He pulled open the door and walked into a dark kitchen lit dimly from the street lights in front.

Details…he reminded himself. He needed to pay attention to details. He removed his shoes, putting them on the mat by the door, to keep the floors clean. The white tile floor felt so hard and cold against the warmth of his stocking feet.

He took his cell phone out of his pocket to use the 'flashlight' app he had installed that day. He held it downward so the light couldn't be seen through the living room windows. He was careful not to touch any surface or door frame as he made his way through the house.

The first door he opened was a powder room decorated in navy blue paint and chrome fixtures. He used a Kleenex from his pocket to open the door knobs to keep from leaving finger prints.

The second door was a small office that had a massive desk tucked in one corner and a pull out couch pushed against one wall. He guessed it was a guest room and office. He again closed the door with the tissue.

Then he saw the open door at the end of the hallway. He took a picture of the door with his phone so he would remember exactly how it was left open. As he walked in, a huge smile spread across his face. The room contained a king sized bed and a large television screen on the far wall. The curtains were pulled tightly shut and he knew he could turn on the set without fear the glare could be seen through the window. What luck! He really missed relaxing with the tube at the end of the day, before he went to sleep.

This was the room he would stay in. He started at one side of the room and took pictures on his phone. He especially took note of how the bed was made, how the corners were tucked and how the pillows were arranged.

A newly remodeled master bath was attached on one side. The travertine tile shower looked so inviting but he vowed to continue using the one at the post office. It was too risky to use all of the amenities in this house. All he really wanted was a good night sleep, a toilet and a little time watching TV to relax.

He unmade the bed all the way down to the mattress protector. He put his own sheets onto the bed and used his own blanket and pillow. He removed his clothes except for his boxers and brushed his teeth in the bathroom. He pulled back the covers and slipped between the cool slick sheets. It felt like heaven to lie down on such a soft mattress again and to relax with a good movie.

He plugged his cell phone in and carefully set his alarm. He wanted to perfectly return everything to exactly the way he had found it and leave before the sun came up. Even though he was getting up very early his night's sleep would be amazing compared to sleeping in his car.

He lay there for a moment trying to think about his situation. How did it come to this? Here he was basically homeless and now a criminal of a misdemeanor. He was so sure Betsy would stay with him no matter what he did. I guess she taught him a lesson that he had already known for years. He always took advantage of every situation. He kept cheating because he thought he could get by with it. He decided right then that he needed to change his ways. This is NOT where he wanted to be at this stage of his life.

But with no other options available he would make the best of his situation. After all, as long as he carefully watched every little detail, what could go wrong?

Chapter #6

The House at 1723 Stoney Point

The alarm scared him when it went off. For a moment he looked around confused until he realized where he was. He rubbed his eyes roughly then looked around the room in the light from the television that had stayed on all night.

He slightly opened the curtain to look out and saw the sun was just edging over the cityscape. The small stream of golden sun lit up the features in the room.

On the wall was a large portrait of an older couple. The gilded frame was elaborately carved and nearly glowed as the sun highlighted it, as if it had a light source of its own.

Both of the people in the portrait had gray hair, though hers was more salt and pepper than his was. They were looking at each other and the look was impossible to mistake. A couple that still loved one another after many decades of marriage. A bond that Peter really couldn't understand, but thought must be a powerful feeling.

There was also a picture of the man when he was much younger. He was smiling, proudly wearing a graduation gown and holding up a certificate stating he had earned his Juris Doctor Law Degree.

Peter was impressed. He slept in the bed of an attorney!

On the other wall were three pictures, two men and a woman. They were obviously the couple's children since the men looked a lot like their father and the woman was undeniably a younger version of her mother. Seeing the people who lived in the house suddenly made him feel uncomfortable as if he was eavesdropping on a private conversation. And he realized he actually was.

There was a triangle shaped frame on the dresser that held an American flag. Beside it was a program from a funeral, his funeral. Peter now knew the Attorney had passed and only his wife was still living in the premises.

Peter did not have any children, anyway, not that he knew of. For a moment, he wondered what it would feel like to smile at your children's picture before you close your eyes each night. He hoped someday that he could experience how that felt.

Peter quickly got dressed in his uniform. He used a towel he 'borrowed' from the sleazy hotel he stayed at for when he showered at the post office. He was so tempted to use the massive shower and the super soft towels in the closet, smelling of fresh air and lavender, but he didn't dare disturb the carefully arranged linens and toiletries in the bathroom closet.

Peter packed up his things and carefully made the bed with the original sheets and blankets. He carefully checked the picture on his phone to make sure he left it looking exactly as he found it, down to the throw pillows that decorated the headboard. Even though he planned on coming back that evening, he felt it was a necessary precaution just in case someone was checking on the house for the owner.

Peter locked the door to the garage as he left since he knew it was easy to open. The sun was just coming up over the roof tops when he edged out of the back garage door. He stayed in the shadow of the house, alert to any activity around the neighborhood, before he made it to the sidewalk and then tried again to walk nonchalantly around the corner to his car.

McDonalds suddenly sounded great for breakfast. He decided to celebrate his good night of sleep…his *free* good night of sleep!

Each day Peter picked up his mail at the post office. He told them he was just making sure nothing got into the hands of his soon to be ex-wife. He let everyone at the office believe he was still staying at the cheap roach motel, and routinely made up stories about hearing noises from the room next door. They all had a good laugh over his miserable situation. He knew it was an important detail to keep his coworkers from suspecting anything.

Each evening he found somewhere to have a simple supper, usually the nightly special at a small diner down the street called Ma's Café. Ma was a full bodied middle aged lady with a loud laugh and a kind heart.

"Could you help me out young man?" she asked one night as he was ready to leave.

"Sure," said Peter willing to help her. "What can I do for you?"

"I guess I made too many pies today and I am stuck with a lot of extra apple pie," she spoke with a sheepish look on her face. "Could I send a piece home with you? No charge of course, I just don't want it to go to waste. You'd be helping me out." And the twinkle in her eye said it all.

"That would be very nice. I love apple pie!" Peter answered her, grateful for her generosity.

"Thank you so much," she said still playing her part. "I'm so glad it has found a good home!" And she loaded an extra large piece into a take home white styrofoam container. "Enjoy your night!"

Peter smiled with appreciation. He had been eyeing the pie in the glass case up front but didn't feel he should splurge just yet. Someday he'd come back and leave her a huge tip for her kindness.

After supper he drove to the neighborhood park and ate his pie sitting on a worn wooden bench while watching the children play and the adults jogging by. He didn't dare go back to the house before dark and even then he drove around a couple of times to make sure there were no lights inside.

On the weekends he did the same routine. He offered to work overtime each Saturday to earn additional money but also because it kept him busy. Sundays got real long. But the lawyers were keeping him busy writing up lists of items that he wanted from the marriage and creating lists of all of their assets. He spent a lot of time sitting at Ma's, eating pie and getting his assignments from his lawyer completed. He still waited until after dark to return to the house.

The owner of the house at Stoney Point was to return soon so he'd have to find a new location to stay. It had been a wonderful place and he would miss the huge TV that hung on the bedroom wall. That had been his only entertainment since he messed up his marriage causing Betsy to kick him out, though for right now it was enough.

Chapter #7

Drake

Peter stood by the long racks of cubicles. He was sorting the outgoing mail and he had several fully packed bags to go through today. The sorting machines were down and all of the mail had to be sorted by hand. It would be a very late night.

"Hi Jerry," Peter said as his boss walked behind him, on his way to his office.

"Oh hi Peter," Jerry said surprised as if he didn't see him standing there. "How's the in town mail going?"

"Actually, I'm almost done. I think I will work on the mail holds next so we don't miss anyone."Peter added, "As long as that is okay with you?"

"I don't care," replied Jerry with a deep sigh. "It all has to be done by 4:00 so I don't care what order, just so it gets done." He hated days when the machines were down. He was frustrated that they couldn't requisite newer equipment so it wouldn't break down as often but he always got the same answer, 'It's not in the budget'. Jerry headed down the aisle toward his office and shut the door behind him.

Peter looked through the bins and sorted the mail to the holds section from his push cart. Most of the mail holds were only for five to seven days-not long enough for him unless he were to get desperate.

"Frank Crawford, 1705 Roosevelt," He read to himself. This address was a new hold as of today. They wanted the mail held for two weeks and it was a pretty nice neighborhood. He wrote it down on a scrap of paper and tucked it into the pocket of his uniform trousers. He would check it out that evening. Technically he had a couple of paychecks behind him now but the payments he had to make to Betsy's lawyer pretty well wiped him out. He had never been responsible for a full half of their bills before since Betsy earned a lot more money than he did. As long as he didn't have to pay for a hotel or apartment he could survive, paycheck to paycheck.

He ate the special at Ma's again and this time she had some chocolate fudge brownies that would be tossed tonight if they weren't eaten. Could he help her out again?

Ma was a saint! She had no idea how special those brownies really were to him. Amazing how he had begun to appreciate even such small acts of kindness.

He spent time sitting in the park again. Many of the neighborhood moms came to the park to wear their kids out before bedtime. Peter shared his bench with a couple of them and they became friends after talking evening after evening. He especially got to know one lady named Pam.

Pam had a little boy that was so excited every night when he got to the park. He was three years old and his name was Drake. His tousled blonde hair and big blue eyes were way too mischievous. He had piles of energy and Peter could see why she needed to wear him out.

"What you name?" Drake asked Peter innocently the first time they met.

"My name is Peter."

"Peeta?" Drake questioned sweetly.

"It's Peter." He said smiling.

"Okay Peeta," Drake said running toward the row of swings. "Come push me Peeta!"

"He really likes you, you know," said Pam. Her dark blonde hair and clear blue eyes were a beautiful contrast to her tanned skin. This was the fifth night in a row that they shared a bench and she enjoyed talking with him. She looked forward to it each day.

"I like him too," Peter admitted cautiously. "I don't have any kids and he makes me wonder if that is what I've been missing in my life." He marveled that Drake was such a complete little person, full of curiosity, in such a tiny energetic package.

They compared notes on ex-husbands and soon to be ex-wives. It seemed that they had both been in mismatched relationships from the beginning.

"Would you come to my house for dinner some night?" Pam inquired quietly. She was hoping he would ask her out but impatiently decided to take the plunge herself. She shyly looked up to see his reaction.

"I would like that," said Peter honestly. "But I want to wait to start dating until my divorce is final. It's been pretty messy so far and I don't want to expose anyone else to my problems. But I would love to see more of you after it is over… I really would." He meant every word of it. He just hoped she wouldn't think it was a brush off.

"I felt that way too when I was getting divorced," Pam said nodding. She absentmindedly twisted a strand of hair that fell down her shoulder with her thumb and first finger. "So I understand."

Peter was relieved because he did look forward to her company. He looked forward to seeing her every day.

Chapter #8

1705 Roosevelt

Peter drove down Roosevelt Street reading the house numbers as he passed them. "1697…1699…1701…1703…1705!"

The house was very dark and the yard was shadowy. Peter drove by slowly then continued down the street trying to see if there was anything to be concerned about.

So far it looked vacant so he parked his car in a hotel parking lot about one block away. He shoved his shaving kit and his sheets, pillow and blanket into his backpacks and zipped them up tight. He headed down the sidewalk aware that the street was brightly lit, maybe a bit too much.

This house was a nice two story with dormers above and an attached garage on the side. He decided it was too risky to go through the garage service door, since it faced the street, so he headed to the back by staying in the tree shadows.

As he slid along the side of the house he came to a chain link fence whose expanse was interrupted by a metal gate, topped with curved metal decorations. He lifted the old metal latch and pulled on the gate. He froze and his heart instantly went into overdrive as the gate protested his plan with a loud grating sound, almost as bad as finger nails on a chalk board. He slipped back into the shadows and waited breathless to see if anyone noticed the gate's unnerving sound. After a few long minutes he started to breathe easier and decided to try it again. He pulled on the gate again but this time he did it so slowly that the grumbling that emitted was of a lower octave, so not as alarming. He would need to borrow some machine oil from work tomorrow to fix his groaning gate problem.

The back of the house had a porch that wound around the corner with white spindles and a hanging porch swing that had definitely seen better days. In the center was a screen door covering a wooden entry door.

The screen door opened easily and quietly. He tried the well worn door knob and found it locked. He pulled the worn red, white and blue lanyard from under his coat. His employee ID card made a larger 'key' than his credit card with so much more to hang on to. As soon as he slid it between the door and the frame he heard a simple click to know he was in.

This time he walked directly into the living room, and he locked the door behind him. With the light assist on his phone he easily found the master bedroom.

This house was not huge but it was absolutely immaculate. Everything appeared clean, though plain and unobtrusive. It was not cluttered with decorations or with small memorabilia. It was simple clean lines, tastefully done.

He dove into the process of photographing every detail. He could see the bed was made with a drill Sergeant's precision. He studied all of the creases and tucks carefully, taking photos as he went. The ends of the pillow cases were creased and folded so tightly you would think they had been ironed in place. He hoped he could recreate this one, but he knew he would have to pay extra special attention to the details to pull this off.

The bathroom was stark white with a huge medicine cabinet running the entire length of the counter and sink.

Curiosity got the best of him and he opened the cabinet door with a tissue. For one moment he could not believe what he saw! Dozens of pill bottles were lined up on the shelves. Some were prescription, others were over the counter. Each one perfectly faced the front of the cabinet with exact spacing between each container so precise that you would have needed a ruler to recreate the display. As he looked at the bottles he started to read the names

Advil…Aleve…Aspirin…Benadryl…and he realized they were in perfect alphabetical order!

As he read down the list he saw there was a medicine for nearly every common complaint plus some he didn't recognize. Was the house's owner a very sick man or was he a hypochondriac? He quickly shut the glass cabinet door. Somehow he feared that even looking at them may disrupt their perfect order and his presence might be known. He brushed his teeth carefully, not to leave even one bubble in the sink.

He stripped the bed down to the mattress protector. He laid the sheets carefully across a chair hoping they wouldn't get even one wrinkle in them. He definitely did not have good ironing skills.

Even though Peter vowed to never touch anything in the other rooms he was compelled to open the pantry door with a tissue in hand. The contents were in strict little rows like soldiers marching to war. The cupboards were the same. Even the silverware drawer had little white labels stating forks, spoons and knives. He decided the person must have some type of compulsive disorder to need to label plates and cups on the edge of each shelf. Or maybe he was crazy!

Peter definitely would need to be careful about touching anything if he didn't have to.

He set his phone alarm for a half hour earlier than usual because it would take longer to make sure he had covered all of his tracks.

The next day at the post office Peter was searching through the tool box looking for machine oil to use on the screechy gate.

"Can I help you?" asked his boss Jerry, obviously annoyed Peter wasn't working on the mail that was stacked around the room.

Peter jerked back so fast he knocked the tool box off of the counter sending tools cascading all over the floor like so many cockroaches when a light is turned on. He dropped down on to his knees to collect the tools and hastily sorted them back into the tool box with clangs of metal on metal.

"Oh, I'm so sorry," said Peter with his cheeks flushed bright pink. "I was looking for that tube of machine oil."

"What do you need it for?" Asked Jerry somewhat panicked. "Don't tell me some equipment broke down again?"

"No...It's...It's my chair." Peter stammered. "It doesn't swivel right so I was going to lube it."

"Well, make sure you get all of the tools back in the box." Jerry said in a commanding voice. "I think I saw an Allen wrench slide under the cabinet."

"I'll get it," said Peter in a pitch higher than he expected. "Don't worry. I'll make sure I have them all." Peter got down on all fours and peered under the counter until he located the concealed wrench, now wrapped in a tangled dust bunny.

Jerry continued down the aisle until he paused at Peter's desk. He reached out with his index finger and touched the back of his chair.   It silently swiveled in place with barely any effort.

"I must have misunderstood," thought Jerry to himself. Peter must have been putting the oil back instead of looking for it. "Whatever," He muttered to himself, "I don't have time for this kind of stuff!"

Peter retrieved all of the tools and put the tool box away in the cabinet. He found the small bottle of oil and slipped it into his pocket to use later. He would return it in the morning and no one would ever need to know it had been borrowed.

Peter was in good spirits as he left work that night. He walked out the backdoor of the warehouse and down the steps to the parking lot with more spring in his step than normal. I guess a good night's sleep was just what he had needed.

A brand new yellow Mustang car was sitting in the parking lot with its motor running. Peter had always dreamed of having a machine like that someday. Its motor purred quietly but he knew the big engine underneath her hood would roar into action with just a touch of the gas pedal. It must be a blast to drive!

The mustang's passenger door opened as Peter walked by on the way to his car. A woman with dark auburn silky hair stepped out smiling and waving a flirty good bye. It was Jenny. Peter guessed this car belonged to the illusive boyfriend. He realized he was in no position to compete with someone that had a possession like that. Money not only talks, it flirts real well too.

Jenny jogged around the car and bounded up the three stairs into the postal warehouse. She hadn't seen Peter walking to his car, and that was a favor to him.

Peter went to eat at Ma's again after work and to his delight received a plate of chocolate chip cookies, that would have 'gone to waste' to share with Pam and Drake at the park. His routine was becoming a pleasant one and he saw that life after divorce could still be enjoyed.

The gate practically drank the machine oil and after a few more squirts he could move the gate without hardly any resistance. He knew in a few hours of soaking it would be effortless and silent.

Peter lie in bed watching an old movie on the flat screen TV. He reached into his duffle bag and unzipped the small compartment on the inside. He pulled out the object and examined it. It was his wedding ring, a simple gold band with both of their initials engraved on the inside.

At one time he felt BJ + PJ written inside meant a promise for a happy future. When Peter put his wedding band on at the ceremony he meant for this union to last forever. At that time he was determined to be faithful and felt they would have a good life together. But he started to get bored of the work/sleep routine. But the real kicker was when his wife was promoted at her job. Betsy had come home bubbling over with joy. She had been promoted to manager of her accounting office and it came with a big increase in pay. No, it was a HUGE increase in pay.

Suddenly Peter was no longer the bread winner of the family. He started to feel like less of a man and Betsy started to take control. She went out and bought the Lexus and put a down payment on the house they were buying. Since the majority of the money came from her paycheck, he got less of a voice in the decisions. Just looking at the ring and feeling the cold metal in his hand made him feel like a failure. He put it on the bed stand beside him because he couldn't stand to look at it and he swore the coldness of it reached to his very bones. He rolled over and finally fell fast asleep.

The next morning, he replaced the sheets and checked his photos to make sure he arranged them correctly. He put the bottle of machine oil into his pocket. He would slip it back into the tool box when everyone was at lunch. The gate now swung with hardly any noise. The plan was perfect.

Peter's day at work was physically hard. The trucks of mail were filled to the brim and all of the employees, along with Peter, had to hustle all day long to get it all processed. Peter's feet were sore and throbbing by the end of his shift.

But the worst part was the headache that started about an hour into the day. It started behind his eyes, blurring his vision until he saw double at times. The old cliché of feeling like your head was in a vice was all to true for him. It definitely wasn't helped by the visitor that came to see him.

"Peter," said Jerry quietly. "Come back to my office. You have a visitor."

"Who?" urged Peter, but Jerry just shook his head and motioned with a quick jerk of his hand that he should follow him.

Sergeant Williams stood stiffly by the side of Jerry's desk. He had an apologetic look on his face but he was still there to do his duty.

"Mr. Johnson…Peter Johnson?"

"Yes, I'm Peter Johnson," said Peter with an annoyed tone to his voice.

The officer held out an envelope and Peter gingerly accepted it.

"You have been legally served." The officer looked at Jerry and nodded. "Excuse me, I'll see myself out," he said to no one in particular. He exited the room quickly.

Peter looked at the envelope in disbelief.

What did she want this time?

He torn the envelope open so fast he got a paper cut from sliding his finger under the flap.

"Ouch!" He exclaimed loudly. "Darn it!" The blood was running down his finger in a bright red stream and dripped onto the contents of the envelope as he unfolded the stiff legal looking document.

"Now she is threatening to take half of my post office retirement!" He closed his eyes tightly and shook his head in total disbelief. He barely had anything left to live on! And now he would probably lose his opportunity to retire early on a full pension. Guess that wasn't going to happen now.

All he wanted to do is go take a hot shower and fall into bed. His body ached from head to toe and his brains seemed to hurt even worse. He couldn't wait for nightfall so he could do just that.

Chapter #9

Murder

"Who are you?" A horrified voice demanded from behind the bathroom door. The voice was old and shaky, raspy and hoarse. "What are you doing in my house?" The man ended the sentence with a loud sobbing sound.

The intruder, wearing a black mask and gloves, swung around and came face to face with an elderly man standing naked in the doorway of the bathroom with only a stark white towel around his waist. He was holding on to the towel ends with both hands. He was shaking from fear and started to gasp for air with deep ragged breaths.

"Who are you?" the old man shrieked. "Why are you in my house?" The elderly man started to run for the front door as fast as he could with a look of pure terror on his face.

The man wearing black chased after him and grabbed his arm roughly. He could feel his bones through his thin skin with little muscle to protect them.

"Let go of me!" Leave me alone!" the old man yelled in a higher pitch then before.

"Please don't hurt me!" He begged as he struggled to get free. He kicked the man in black in the shins repeatedly, but the man was not loosening his grip. He tried to pull at his mask but the man was tall and he couldn't get it off.

"I won't hurt you. Just calm down...NOW!" said the masked man. They ended up wrestling and the elderly man landed face down on the floor as he tried to free himself, his arm wrenched behind him as he fell.

"Help...me! Help! Don't... hurt... me!" He gasped, completely out of air, struggling for every breath.

"Please... leave me... alone!" The old man started to gurgle as he spoke. The more he gurgled, the less he fought back.

"Hey mister!" the man with the mask demanded. "I won't hurt you! Just lie down and quit fighting me!"

The old man kept struggling as much as he could. He kept trying to pull away and kicked the intruder in the shins again and again. He was breathing with a raspy airy sound as if inhaling was very painful and becoming nearly impossible to do. But he gave one more big push against the masked man and he stood up free for a fleeting moment. But jerking backwards caused him to hit the back of his head sharply against the corner of the hard oak cabinets.

The old man slowly melted to the floor with a bone on wood sound, and stopped motionless. The masked man rolled him over to see pale skin and eyes that were wide open but were rolled upward into his eye sockets. Blood trickled down from the gaping wound on the back of his head and mixed with his thinning grey hair.

"Mister? Are you okay?" The man in black demanded. "Are you okay?"

Another intruder, wearing a brown mask and gloves came out of the bedroom with a big screen TV in his arms. "What's going on?" He asked shocked at the scene in front of him.

"I think he's dead!" The first man said as he removed his gloves and held his two fingers against the man's neck. "I can't find a pulse!"

"Let's get out of here!" Said the brown masked man urgently, "We have enough. Let's go!"

The black masked man stood up, his hands shaking as he replaced his gloves, from the realization of what had just happened.

"Don't die old man! We weren't going to hurt you! It was an accident!" He looked back and he could see the pool of thick red blood growing underneath the man's head. He grabbed a hold of one end of the big screen TV and helped the other man carry it out of the door as fast as they possibly could. Together they fled out into the shadows crossing the lawn quietly. If the old man survived he wouldn't be able to identify them because of their masks. Their identities were safe either way.

Peter held on tight to his duffle bag and blankets. He was conscious of every step he took trying to be quiet, but still wanted to walk naturally to stay inconspicuous. As he came around the side of the house he caught movement in the shadows of the trees in the backyard. He froze behind a large tree, frightful of being seen and hoping they couldn't hear his heart pounding in his chest like a big old kettle drum. He molded against the tree so tightly that he ended up with rough bark indents on his cheek. He feared the owners had returned but after peeking around the tree he realized that probably was not the case.

He saw two men carrying a flat screen television set across the backyard battling the brisk breeze. It wasn't just any flat screen…it was *his* flat screen! The one he was hoping to watch tonight before going to sleep.

He watched as they maneuvered it through the now silent gate and continued across the lawn. The men loaded it into the back of a van, parked by the street, just out of the reach of the street lights. The van was white with a logo of some sort on the passenger door. He couldn't read it but he could see the picture. It was a drawing of a large mosquito with big buggy eyes and long sprawling legs. He could make it out even in the darkness since it was on a white background.

They loaded up a few more previously collected articles that were lying in the grass by the street. They swiftly jumped in the van, driving at first with no lights on. Peter saw the lights flip on at the first stop sign. They then quietly disappeared down the street driving normally, like nothing ever happened.

That was close! Peter could have walked in on them!   Unfortunately he knew he would need to find a new place to stay. It would be too risky to stay here now. The thieves might return for another load.

He decided to go inside to see what had been taken out of some morbid curiosity. He made his way across the wet lawn, concealed in the shadows, and saw that the back door was wide open and was swinging freely in the wind.

He poked his head around the door frame gingerly, afraid of being seen in case the masked men had more partners. He stretched his neck to see further into the room. Instead of thieves he saw a man laying flat on the floor, face up. His face was the color of death. His eyes were glassy and vacant. And the pool of bright red blood was now the size of a basketball and growing.

Peter hurried to his side and knelt down. He put two fingers to the side of the man's neck. No pulse. He checked the position of his neck to open his airway and titled his chin upward as he had been taught in countless sessions of CPR classes. Then he put his ear to the man's chest to listen for breathing. He decided to start compressions. He knew the new requirements for CPR had changed to worrying about circulation first. Peter started doing compressions, hands locked on top of the man's breastbone and he started his up and down motion while kneeling beside him. After a few minutes he realized it didn't seem to be helping since he saw no response from the elderly man.

Instinctively Peter started doing some rescue breaths. The old man tasted like minty toothpaste. Peter was on breath number nine and he still saw no results. He checked for a pulse but could not find one.

The siren coming down the street suddenly became louder. He realized in horror that it was coming down Roosevelt Street.

"Sorry, old man…I tried." He mumbled to the body lying before him as he stood up and slipped out the back door and took refuge in the dark shadows again.

The walk to his car seemed to take longer than he'd remembered. Every cautious step was at least a minute long in his mind. As he turned the corner he saw the police car lights blinking over the top of the house. Someone must have called in because they saw something. He knew it was possible the something they saw was him. He wanted to call the ambulance but he was sure the man was dead so it would not have helped anyhow.

The policeman knocked on the front door of the house. "Hello! Are you okay?" When he didn't receive a response he hurried to the back yard and through the metal gate. He carefully headed to the open back door drawing his gun as he stealthily walked.

The officer saw the body but expertly checked all of the rooms for intruders, keeping his gun cocked and ready. When satisfied he was alone, the officer knelt down and felt the man's pulse. He unsnapped his radio from his belt. "I need a rescue unit at 1705 Roosevelt. I have an elderly white male that is unresponsive and does not have a pulse. I am starting CPR."

Before he finished the call, another officer entered through the back door. He held a medical kit in one hand and had his gun drawn in the other.

"It's clear," Announced the first officer. The second officer secured his gun in his holster and together they placed a small mask on the man's face and started the CPR process. They would continue until the rescue unit arrived.

Peter heard the red rescue unit coming long before he saw the chaos of dancing lights. He was back in his car, heading to the grocery store parking lot, ready to bed down for a fitful night's sleep.

Peter kept thinking through all of the events of that night. So many things happened in such a short span of time. As he lay there, crumpled up in the back seat of his car, he rubbed his cold hands together. He noticed the tan free strip around his third finger and realized that he no longer had his wedding ring. He had left it on the table beside the bed the night before.

Chapter #10

The Ring

Sleep didn't come easy, and actually it came hardly at all. He worried through the night about his ring on the bedside table and if the man lived or died.

It was nearly dawn when he decided to drive past the house on Roosevelt to see what was happening.

Three black and white police cars were parked in front of the house. One car announced on its door that it belonged to a detective. A white coroners van was sitting in the driveway by the garage door. A gurney was being wheeled down the driveway. It held a large black vinyl bag that was shaped like a person. The old man had died.

One man was pulling the gurney and a woman was behind pushing it. They opened the back of the coroners van and after folding the front legs back it was a simple lift and push to slide it inside.

Peter could feel the goose bumps rising on the back of his neck and the beads of sweat popping out on his forehead. He started to breathe in short deep breaths and couldn't help but panic.

In the back yard two male officers were combing the area looking for clues. They stopped to take photos of the ground at times and they picked up things to put into plastic zip lock bags. He knew he didn't hurt the old man but he was terrified to have been on the scene. He worried the police investigators may find something to connect him to this house.

Just then a car came wildly flying down the street toward him. Both of the people in the car were so intently looking at the house and the police activity that they veered into Peter's lane. They would have crashed head on if Peter hadn't had the awareness to hit his horn with the palm of his hand and swerve into a parking spot on the side of the road to avoid them.

The driver suddenly was aware of him and cranked the wheel the other direction, mouthing the words, "Sorry."

The car had a logo on the door. KRCC NEWS.

"Oh great!" thought Peter, "News coverage." But at least he could keep up on the story listening to the radio since he was temporarily without a TV to watch.

Peter watched in his rear view mirror as the car's passenger, a slender young blonde lady, got out of the car and hurried up to the

Coroner's van, tiptoeing with her extremely high heels, microphone in hand. Her driver, a graying black man in his fifties, parked the car and hustled to keep up with her, camera already taping.

Peter quickly tried to find channel KRCC on his car radio. They were airing live.

"Here we are at 1705 Roosevelt Drive where a man was found dead in his home earlier this morning. The cause of death is still unknown.   The death is being investigated and is being treated as a homicide pending the results of an autopsy. The identity of the victim is not being released until notification of next of kin. We will have more on this story as it unfolds. This is Donna Reynolds reporting for KRCC TV."

Peter sat frozen in his car seat. Homicide! Having heard the word spoken out loud caused him to feel sick to his stomach instantly. If only he had not been there!

He decided to go in to work early so he could shower and shave in the employee break room. This also gave him a chance to return the small bottle of machine oil to its place in the tool box.

The shower did wonders to wake him up and calm his nerves. He drank a couple of black cups of coffee to prepare himself for the day. He wished he had called the police when he saw the bandits, but it was too late now. His delay would make him look guilty, though he wasn't sure of exactly what.

He was sure it would seem like a very long day.

Chapter #11

Sheila Crawford

Sheila walked around her father's house with tears in her large brown eyes. Since she lived closest out of her siblings, she was always the one that looked out for their Dad. Now she would have the task of disposing of his things and of selling the house. It seemed like a daunting task at this point.

Having someone murder her father made no sense at all. He had been retired for several years and never had an unkind word to say. It seemed like a bad dream that you couldn't wake up from.

Detective Martin instructed her that the entire house was being considered a crime scene. She was not allowed to touch anything or any surface in the house. Her job was to try to identify what was missing or disturbed.

Her father was a wonderful parent but he was a hypochondriac and had a compulsive disorder. Every detail of this house had remained the same, <u>exactly</u> the same, since her mother had passed away. This made it easy for her to observe what had been taken.

Sheila went into the stark white bathroom and used a tissue to open the cabinet door. Not a single spot was empty and the bottles were still in alphabetical order. This really puzzled the detectives and police officers since pharmaceuticals were the number one item stolen in this community. Normally this cabinet would have been cleaned out first. Since her father was found wearing a towel they are assuming her father had been in the bathroom which deterred the thieves.

Sheila's father called her the day before saying he was cutting his vacation short because he wasn't feeling very well. He was home resting and she was going to come by today to check on him. She offered to come over last night but her father was very proud of being independent and talked her out of it. "I just need some rest," is all he would say. She so wished she would have driven over to see him anyhow. Now she would never have that chance again.

Sheila made note of the flat screen TV set that was unbolted from the bedroom wall. Also of the jewelry box that was missing from his dresser and his lap top computer and tv from the small office.

Sheila felt like she needed some fresh air so she went to the back yard. She had cried for several hours after being notified of his death. It was horrible to go down to the coroner's office to identify his body. She had cried so hysterically there that she didn't seem to have tears left right now. But she was sure she would find them many times again in the days ahead.

The police told her that the garage service door was unlocked but that wasn't unusual. Her father rarely locked it.

She walked around the side of the house and lifted the latch on the gate and swung it open. She stopped in her tracks, confused. She gingerly swung the gate back and forth again, still with hardly any effort and with no sound. For as long as she could remember this gate opened hard and screeched at every inch! Her Dad referred to it as his secret security alarm. The truth was he refused to use chemicals like oils on his lawn or garden because he worried it would contaminate the soil or it may kill the grass.

She noticed a circle of moisture around the bottom of the hinged post. She reached down with her index finger and touched the oily substance. She had no idea why someone would oil the hinges but she knew for sure it was not her father.

Chapter #12

The squeaky garden gate

Sergeant Williams sat in his large leather chair behind his messy, but organized, desk. The man wore a blue officer's uniform with the buttons bulging because of his girth. He had long bristly eyebrows that always seem to have a few stragglers that curled down in front of his eyes.

He instinctively reached over to pick up the phone from its receiver, as he heard the first ring.

"Sergeant Williams."

"Hi, Sergeant Williams," a hesitant female voice said, "This is Sheila Crawford."

"Oh, hello Sheila. We here at the police department are so saddened to hear about your father. Are you doing okay?"

"I'm doing okay considering the situation," Sheila continued sniffing softly. "I just walked through my father's house and wanted to let you know what I saw."

"I know this is a very hard time but we really appreciate your help in figuring out what happened." The Sergeant sounded very sincere.

"Most things were exactly as they have been since my mother passed away. My father felt it preserved my Mom's memory by keeping things precisely as she had arranged them. In fact, I moved a plant once to give it more sunlight and my father immediately moved it back. He said it was comforting for him to keep things the same and that it helped him deal with losing her."

"He sounds like a sensitive man."

"Yes he was," agreed Sheila sadly, slowly nodding her head.

"He was very devoted to my Mother," But she realized she needed to get to the reason why she called. "I just wanted you to know I left a list of missing items with the detective that was on site."

"Thank you very much," the Sergeant answered running his fingers through his salt and pepper hair. "I know this is hard but any information could make the difference. Please let us know if you think of anything else. You can reach me at any time."

"Well there was one thing that was weird," she admitted hesitantly. "But I doubt it is very important."

"You never know…sometimes the smallest detail can make or break a case." He added, "What did you see?"

"Well." She paused thoughtfully. "Someone oiled the gate to the back yard."

"Why do you think that?" The Sergeant asked curiously, raising his shaggy eyebrows as he asked the question.

"Because ever since my parents bought that house the metal gate in back screeches loudly whenever it is opened. But now it makes no noise at all and I noticed there is a small pool of oil down on the grass and leaves below the hinges." Sheila started to feel silly bringing up such trivial information, but he did say to report everything and anything.

"And my Dad never used oils or chemicals because he was constantly nervous about contamination to the soil, so I am positive he did not apply the oil."

"Thank you, Sheila," The Sergeant said. "I will check it out and make note of it."

After he hung up the phone he closed his eyes, crossed his big muscular arms and leaned way back in his chair, slowly rocking as he thought.

"Why would someone oil a rusty old gate? Was it to come and go unnoticed?" Since people don't normally walk around with oil in their pockets, this meant one thing. If it is proven that Mr. Crawford was indeed murdered, then planning ahead by oiling the gate could mean it was *premeditated* murder, a *much* stiffer charge.

He grabbed his police hat off of the hook and headed down the hall to his police car waiting outside. He checked the supply of empty glass vials that he kept in his glove compartment. He decided to go over and get a sample of the oil if it was still there. It was to rain later that day so it would need to be collected now.

He also had his fingerprint kit with him. The house had been completely dusted but he doubted they would have checked the gate or the hinged pole.

Chapter #13

Emmet Street House

Peter had a very long day, even worse than he anticipated. The sorting machines broke down so he had to work extra hours to finish the huge bags of mail that came that day. He also received his first lawyer's bill. Two thousand dollars and he had no savings. He needed to scrimp every where possible.

When he got off work he headed to Ma's to have some supper. Tonight Ma wasn't there so he didn't get a desert treat to take to the park to share with Drake and Pam. Talking with them was a nice diversion from the troubles he faced. Drake entertained him by showing him his cart wheel that he had learned in daycare. Peter and Pam laughed until their stomachs hurt as he flipped head over heels, and often landed in a giggling heap on the ground.

After they left the park Peter wasn't sure where to go. But he figured the cheap hotel was his best bet.

As Peter drove down the street to the older part of the town he noticed the street sign that said Emmet Street to his left. He opened his glove compartment and pulled out the list of holds, remembering there was one listed on that street. His car seemed to have a mind of its own and before he knew it he was driving past the small ranch house with the blue shutters. He could not see any alarm postings and no motion detecting lights. He drove past two more times waiting to see if lights would go on inside. When it stayed dark he decided it would be safe. He parked two blocks to the north, chosen because the streets were lined with a lot of trees and few street lights.

He walked, trying to look nonchalant. After his experience the night before he almost lost his nerve but the yearning for a good night's sleep pulled strongly on him, also the debt that he had to pay off.

The back door wasn't locked. He decided that was just like receiving an invitation to come on in.

The Emmet Street house was a mess. Dishes were piled high in the sink smelling of spoiled food, clothes were lying on the floor of the bedroom in a heap in the corner and the bathroom definitely needed a scrubbing. The bed wasn't made so it was easy to pull the covers off and replace them with the set of sheets he brought with him He seriously didn't think anyone would have a clue he had even been there. Things were in such disarray.

It was supposed to be empty for three weeks according to the mail hold information. That savings would pay a lot of his lawyer bill. And the bonus was a large flat screen TV in the bedroom. He realized with a chuckle that his needs had become so simple!

When Sergeant Williams returned to his desk that Friday, he found in the center of his desk, several reports relating to the Frank Crawford case.

The lab ran tests on the vial containing the machine oil that he found at the bottom of the gate pole. The results were that it was your average machine oil, Acer Brand, sold at almost every discount and hardware store in town. So it was of no help.

There ended up being three different sets of finger prints on the gate pole. One thumb print belonged to one of the police officers that were on the scene that night. Another print was identified as Sheila Crawford, probably from when she opened the gate that day. A third set was run through the local FBI data base to find an owner. When it came back it showed it was a print from a man named Peter Johnson who worked at the main post office.

Sergeant Williams scratched his head. After serving this man papers so many times he immediately knew who he was. All government workers had to be finger printed to get postal service jobs which meant they were all in the system. It was not unusual for a postal worker to have their finger prints show up at a crime scene. After all they delivered to almost every home in town. So the Sergeant kept an open mind.

Chapter #14

Jerry Posia

As the Sergeant entered the metal double doors the lady behind the counter remarked, "Oh," You could see recognition set in based on the look on her face. "Hi, may I help you?"

"Hello," He said flipping open his badge to prove his identification. "Is Jerry Posia available for me to speak to?"

"Let me ring his office and find out," She paused holding the phone receiver in her hand. "You have been here before but I do not recall your name. Whom shall I say is calling?"

"My name is Sergeant Williams. He will recognize my name."

"His line is busy but I can go back and let him know you are here.

"That would be great. Can I have a seat while I wait for him?" He gestured to a row of chairs against the wall of the lobby.

"Yes. And I will go get Mr. Posia." And she headed back behind some shelves of packaging and he could hear her heels clicking on the cement floor.

In a few moments, softer heels shuffled their way back to the front. A shorter heavy set man with a balding head extended his hand and said, "Jerry Posia." Jerry nervously addressed the Officer, "Nice to see you again."

"Hello, would you have a few minutes for me to ask you a few questions?" The Sergeant asked, "In private if possible."

"Yes Sir," replied Jerry. "Come back to my office." And he turned and led the way.

As the Sergeant followed Jerry back to his office he quickly accessed the area. Multiple shelves with packages and mail lined the walkway. It all seemed very organized and efficient. In the back, machines were sorting envelopes, hundreds of them, by zip code. The machines made a soft whirring sound as letters slid off of a conveyor belt to their prospective bin.

Sergeant Williams was impressed with how quiet but quickly the machines ran. He also noted that a computer screen was scanning and recording every address. It listed the addresses so fast that the screen appeared to blink continually from updates.

"Quite the machines," commented the Sergeant in admiration.

"Yes they are!" replied Jerry. "If it wasn't for them I would need a lot more employees and probably more mail would get misrouted."

The Sergeant walked past the mail holds and was surprised to see so many bins with mail. He remembered getting an explanation of how they functioned at his last visit. Lots of people on vacation he guessed.

They arrived in the office and Jerry motioned to the Sergeant to be seated in either of the chairs sitting in front of his massive metal desk. Jerry then took his place in the worn leather chair behind it.

"So what can I do for you today?" asked Jerry still curious about why the Sergeant was here.

"I'm inquiring about an employee of yours." The Sergeant paused to take a pad of paper and pen out of his attaché case. "I've been here to see him before…It's Peter Johnson."

"Oh my!" Said Jerry shaking his head, "What papers is his wife serving to him this time?"

"I need to ask you a few questions," The Sergeant continued quietly "What is Peter's job position here at the post office?"

"As a full time employee he has a lot of responsibilities and one of them is to fill in on all duties of the office." Jerry took a deep breath and continued, "He fills in at the front counter, he helps load and unload trucks, he sorts and bags mail," His eyes roll upward as he's trying to think of all of things that need to be done.

"He also sweeps the floors, takes out the trash as needed and is in charge of the mail holds as requested by our customers. He also helps do maintenance on the machinery." Jerry kept thinking then ended with, "And any and all other duties as assigned as it states on his job description."

"Does Peter ever deliver mail to residential houses?" Since the duty list was so extensive he was surprised that delivery wasn't included.

"He has filled in for mail carriers in the past but we recently hired a floater carrier that fills in when needed so it hasn't been necessary for quite some time.

"But he has delivered to households in the recent past?"

"I think the last time was probably two months ago but I can get you an exact date, if you need it," Stated Jerry starting to worry what this was all about.

"I appreciate all of your cooperation and information and I'll call you if I have more concerns." Then he added, "I would also appreciate it if you would keep this to yourself and not discuss my visit with Peter. There's no reason for him to become concerned when it's probably not anything."

"I understand," replied Jerry even more anxious than before. "He has enough to worry about already with his pending divorce proceedings. I will keep it to myself."

As the Sergeant walked out of Jerry's office he was wondering to himself how long an oily fingerprint could survive on a metal gate exposed to the elements. He made a mental note to check with an expert as soon as he got back to the office.

"Thank you for your time." The Sergeant extended his hand to Jerry to shake.

"Glad to be able to help." Then Jerry added thoughtfully, "Do I need to be worried about having Peter work here?"

"Oh no, we are still doing fact finding and he is not considered a suspect at this time." The Sergeant concluded. "We are not sure he is connected in any way but we are always thorough and check out every angle."

Jerry's phone started to ring loudly. The Sergeant said as he rose from the chair, "Thank you for your time. I can find my way out."

As the Sergeant walked past the mail sorting machines he noticed a small bottle sitting on the counter. He paused to pick it up. It was machine oil...Acer brand. Was it a coincidence? His reports did say it was extremely common. But he decided to list Peter Johnson as a 'person of interest.'

Chapter #15

Donna Reynolds

When Sergeant Williams entered the police station he nodded a quick 'hello' to the female officer behind the desk. She was listening to someone on the phone and she held up her hand to signal to him to wait for her to complete her call.

"Okay, I will tell him. Thank you." She hung up the phone and said to the Sergeant, "That was the Coroner's Office. He knew you were getting anxious to hear the autopsy results on the Frank Crawford case. He wanted me to tell you he just sent a courier with the results to you." She ended with a big smile. "He should be here shortly."

"Thank you Kristy. I have been anxious to find out what his assessment is."

Whenever he came in to the police station lobby he enjoyed a few minutes talking to Kristy. She was in her forties but wore her age very well on her full figured body. She had a sweet disposition and her generous smile and long caramel hair accented her hazel eyes. He appreciated getting to see her each time he walked in and out of the building. If he was having a frustrating day, her smile always perked him up. Seeing her made him stand up a little straighter and hold his stomach in a little tighter.

Even though he was interested in her, he knew the office required that he maintain professional decorum. Some day he would ask her out but he wasn't positive she would say yes, and he wasn't sure he could handle it if she said no. So it has remained status quo. Though he hoped he would gain the courage someday.

Sergeant Williams was seated at his massive desk, contemplating evidence reports, when someone knocked on his door.

"Come in," he said calmly.

"Courier Sir," Kristy said and she stepped out of the way to let the young man enter the office. He was carrying a flat manila envelope under his arm and held an electronic signature tablet in his hands.

"Could I get a signature, please?"

The Sergeant signed where designated. He hated these electronic machines but understood the need for confidentiality. His signature never came out looking like his normal one did. He took the package and looked at it quickly. It was the coroner's report.

As soon as the courier was out of the door he used his metal letter opener to slice open the end of the envelope. Coroner's reports were very complicated documents, filled with medical mumbo jumbo and lots of numbers with way too many decimals. He had learned the best way to read a coroner's report was to go to the very last page and find the section with the heading of 'conclusion.'

"I conclude, from my extensive research, that Mr. Frank Crawford died from a sharp blow fracturing the occipital bone on the back of his head. He would have been rendered unconscious and the injury, along with the internal bleeding it would have caused, resulted in death."

Sergeant Williams sat back and locked his arms across his chest.

"Hmmmm," he said weighing the facts. He now needed to make this case his top priority. It would now be considered premeditated murder.

He continued reading the conclusion notes.

"Two sets of DNA were discovered on the victim's mouth. Please advise if a federal search is required."

Sergeant Williams picked up his phone and dialed. "I need to speak to the coroner please." He ordered the DNA samples to be run through the registries.

Peter decided to walk to work this morning. It was only four blocks which was only two additional blocks from where his car was parked. Life was less stressful staying at this current house. Since it was already a messy house he didn't stress out as much about trying to cover his tracks.

Last night, as he watched the news on TV, he saw the blonde female reporter giving an update about the Frank Crawford case. Donna, as always, was dressed to the hilt in a dark red dress with tall black heels. She seemed very comfortable in front of the cameras and always seemed excited to report on the news, even on stories that were rather gruesome.

"This is Donna Reynolds reporting for KRCC TV. We want to give you an update on the death of Frank Crawford who resided at 1705 Roosevelt. The coroner has now upgraded the case to premeditated murder. Several suspects are being investigated. Stay tuned to KRCC TV for more updates as they become available. This is Donna Reynolds reporting."

Chapter #16

Report results

"Here's your report, Sergeant," said Kristy smiling brightly at the man behind the desk. "The courier dropped it off while you were gone so I signed for it."

Kristy wore her tailored red blouse because the Sergeant commented once that he thought the red color looked really nice on her. But today he was deep in thought and immediately tore open the envelope containing the DNA report. He didn't even look up at her in his hurry to reach for the package and find out its contents.

He flipped through the pages of the report until he found the conclusion.

"Blah, blah, blah…oh here we go," He said quickly scanning the report.

The Sergeant sat completely still as he read the two names on the report. The first one was expected…Frank Crawford. The second was not expected…Peter Johnson.

"Is everything okay?" Asked Kristy with a concerned look on her face and her brows creased downward.

"The postal worker again!" The Sergeant thought to himself, closing his eyes in disbelief. He had run an extensive background check on Peter. Except for some recent dealings with his wife his record didn't even have a speeding ticket. And now, it seems, he was giving CPR to a dead man. The Sergeant always thought he was a good judge of character but it appears he was wrong this time.

"Kristy, rerun a background check on this man," he said as he quickly jotted the name down on a piece of paper and handed it to her.

Kristy was disappointed that the Sergeant did not notice she was wearing her red blouse. But she took the paper and headed out of the door, back to her desk in front.

Work always was the Sergeants first priority. That's probably why he was promoted to Sergeant and that's probably why he was still single.

Chapter #17

Maybe you should call the police instead

Peter stopped after work at Ma's for supper. He enjoyed the special again, a thick juicy slab of ham and a baked potato with all of the fixings, cheese, bacon, sour cream and a gob of butter on top. And the best part was the big piece of sweet cinnamon peach pie that was sent home so it 'wouldn't go to waste.'

He exited out of the door to the restaurant, feeling exceptionally full now that he was standing upright and started to look around for his parked car.

A vehicle in the parking lot caught his attention and he instinctively stepped back into the shadowy cover of the restaurant's front entryway. He peered around the door frame carefully as the white van backed out of its parking spot and eased out onto the street, turning slowly to the right. As the white van turned he saw the mosquito sticker on the side door.

Jerry had quietly confided in him that the Sergeant had been at the post office asking questions. He pressed Peter to tell him what was going on, but Peter maintained he was innocent and that he had no idea what their inquiry was about.

"It probably has something to do with my *almost* ex-wife," Peter said knowing that could be a very believable lie.

"Just when I thought she had served me every paper there was, I guess she found one more." Peter knew his cheeks were flushed and he hoped Jerry wouldn't notice. Except for his wedding ring he couldn't think of any reason anyone would think he had been there. Unless someone saw him leave the house that night. That he could not be sure about.

After the van turned the corner Peter jogged over to his car and got in to follow it. He had no idea how close or far away to stay behind the van. He hoped they were amateur thieves so maybe they weren't observant enough to know someone was following them.

The van wound around the streets of the town just as it was starting to get real dark outside. Peter traced their path, turn for turn, until he realized they were driving in circles. He thought maybe they were scouting out a house to rob.

As he followed, Peter was thinking about his decision to stay quiet after seeing the thieves that night at the Roosevelt house. He had been afraid that his sleeping arrangements would be discovered, and the last thing he needed was more trouble. But if he could go to the police with information about the crooks maybe they would forgive him his indiscretion. Or at least go real easy on him.

The van started to circle the block again, the very block that Peter was staying at. Each time they passed the Emmet Street house Peter could see the dark forms in the van all peering out the window toward the house! And the van would slow to a crawl. What were the odds that they would be staking out the same house he was staying at…again!

The old van, with the bulging eye mosquito sticker, pulled into a parallel parking spot, in the darkness provided by a huge oak tree. The trees massive branches extended over the cement street. They cut the engine and turned off the lights and sat in silence and darkness. Peter decided to continue driving down the street so as not to raise suspicion. He resisted the impulse to glance at them as he drove by. When he arrived at the corner, he stopped at the stop sign then turned left. As soon as he was hidden by the houses of the neighborhood side street he steered to the curb and parked. He also stayed sitting in silence and darkness.

Peter had gotten quite comfortable staying at the messy Emmet Street house. So comfortable, in fact, that he hadn't been as careful about handling things in the household. He knew his fingerprints were everywhere in the bedroom and the bathroom.

Fear and a measure of curiosity got the best of him. He cracked open the car door hoping no one would hear the metallic sound. He closed the door, after stepping out, but did not shut it all the way. Peter didn't want to risk any more tell tale noises.

He sneaked around the corner, making sure to stay hidden but tried not to look too conspicuous to anyone that might see him from the street or from a homeowner taking an accidental glance through a window shade.

In the yard behind the Emmet Street house he saw a dark figure, completely in black including a face mask. The person was carrying a desk top computer and had a small black knapsack hung over his shoulder. The cloaked figure calmly walked to the van and deposited his treasures in the back end, carefully opening and closing the double door to make as little noise as possible.

Two other dark figures came hurrying out from the house, each with their arms loaded with items they obviously felt were valuable enough to risk getting caught for.

They stored those items into the back of the van and the two of them climbed into the back, closing the double metal doors behind them softly. The last dark figure hurried to the driver's side and, leaving the lights off, drove to the corner and turned to the right.

A police car suddenly turned its headlights on and started its sirens wailing. Peter jerked in response, totally unaware the car had come down the street. It must have traveled so quietly he didn't have any idea they were there.

Peter tucked himself back behind a lilac bush, dropped down onto his knees and watched motionless as the police car revved up its engine and roared into the house's driveway. Peter decided it was time for him to leave. As he stood up shakily to escape to his car he turned and looked straight into a pair of dark eyes, a gleaming badge and the barrel end of a powerful looking forty four.

"Put your hands up!" The officer's deep voice demanded. "Stay on your knees!"

Peter stayed frozen for a long second and then started to babble.

"Sir…Please…My name is Peter Johnson." He started to fumble for his Postal Worker ID. As he reached into his coat pocket the Officer pulled a Stun gun off of his belt and in one swift move, fired the electric device right at Peter.

Peter heard the static of the stun gun before he felt the pain. At first he felt like his brains were scrambled like eggs frying on the top of his skull. He couldn't breathe and his mind totally went blank. Down he went onto the damp grass, his body twitching and twisting.

He landed face down and slammed his nose into the dirt time and time again as convulsions racked his body. He fought to gain control of his movements but he was like a marionette with the electricity controlling his every move.

As Peter started to lose consciousness he noticed the amount of blood smeared on the grass was like a crazy modern painting. The officer jumped to straddle his back and roughly pulled his arms behind him, securing them tightly with a plastic zip strip. The sharp narrow strip was pulled so tightly that it dug deeply into his wrists and cut off his circulation.

Finally the taser stopped shocking him and his brain was starting to clear. "Why are you hurting me?" He found that searching his mind for every word was difficult. He finally stuttered, "I didn't do...do anything wrong!"

"Were you inside this residence robbing the place?" The officer screamed in his ear. "Were you inside this house?"

"Yes," Peter admitted weakly, "but not to rob it...and not tonight! The people in the mosquito van were...were robbing it, not me!"

Peter was crying now, partially because of the intense pain of his bleeding nose and partially due to a feeling of helplessness. The officer pulled him to his feet and escorted him roughly to the waiting police car. They forced his head down as they pushed him into the barred backseat and slammed the door shut.

Peter sank into the seat defeated. He knew there was nothing he could do or say at this point. Plus his brain wasn't working well enough for him to think his situation through.

He tried to wipe the blood off of his face, but with his hands tied behind his back, his only option was his shoulder. Which he soon discovered was insufficient so he gave up and let the blood ooze down his chin and onto his shirt and lap below. He sat silently as if in shock, with his nose throbbing in pain. He sadly looked out the window and noticed a car coming quietly down the street. Thrill seekers, can't resist seeing someone in trouble.

The car drove by slowly. As it drove underneath the halo of the street light, its color caught Peter's eye. It was a yellow Mustang driven by a girl with long auburn silky hair and her boyfriend. It was Jenny from the post office.

Chapter #18

Arrested!

The last time Peter was finger printed was as a requirement for his postal worker job. He thought it was a joke then, but this was no joke this time.

Then it was time for mug shots. They gave him a wet paper towel to wash his face. The blood was dry and it took several scrubbings to get it all off. He supposed the police didn't want the public to see his face as it was, someone would probably yell police brutality. The good thing about it was he finally, after a few minutes of tin snips and cutting, was free from those plastic hand cuffs. The blood could return to his fingers again and it did so through the prickly numbness of circulation cut short for far too long.

When he finally had his face cleaned up he was told to stand in front of a screen containing a massive ruler.

Stand looking forward. Give me a side view, now the other side. And finally he was done and was settled into an interrogation room where they gave him a paper cup half filled with water to drink. Peter was left sitting on a hard metal chair for hours. He had lost track of how many, or did it just seem like hours? He knew it was somewhere in the middle of the night since he could see it was still dark out through the tiny slit of a window above him. But that was all he knew for sure. He wished they would open that window. He felt like the air in the room was thick, heavy and musty smelling. Some fresh air to breathe would have helped him clear the rest of the cobwebs from his still foggy mind.

He studied the glass wall that covered one side of the little claustrophobic room. He knew people were probably behind the two-way mirror looking back at him, studying him, anyway that was how it worked in the police driven TV shows he liked to watch. He had cooperated with every request they made of him because he was not willing to be stunned again. His thoughts were becoming more organized and frankly he didn't know if he could handle the voltage a second time.

The metal door opened with a loud creak and in walked the officer who used the stun gun on him. Behind him entered Sergeant Williams, who took a chair in the back corner, a comfy chair with a soft back and seat.

"Peter Johnson," The officer started flipping through some papers on a clip board. "Is that your real name?"

"Well of course it is." Peter answered. "I was trying to tell you that when you shot me with the stun gun." He said rubbing his hand on his chest. "That hurts by the way."

"You weren't following directions." The officer continued grimly, "You looked like you were reaching for a gun."

"But I wasn't!" Peter pleaded. "If you would have listened to me you would have been able to catch the thieves. They pulled around the corner right before you drove up!"

"Are you ready to give us the names of your accomplices?" The officer said. "We can go a lot easier on you if you help us solve this case."

"I don't have accomplices!" Peter argued, turning beet red from the effort to control himself. "You need to find the guys in the white mosquito van. I drove by and saw three people carrying things out of the house and so I pulled around the corner to see what was happening. "

"That's interesting," said the officer smugly. "We dusted the house for prints and guess what we found?"

Peter slouched down in the hard back chair. His stomach did a few back somersaults and he felt acid rise up in his throat. He knew exactly what they found. He said softly, "You found my finger prints."

"What?" said the officer, "Speak up!"

"You found my prints in the house," Peter repeated softly.

"WHAT?" demanded the officer again. He yelled it at Peter while leaning across the desk. He was so close that Peter could smell black coffee on his breath and the stench did not help Peter's nauseous stomach at all.

"You found my prints in the house!" Peter yelled as loud as he could.

"Yes we did." Said the officer, confident he had the evidence needed to convict his suspect. "How can you explain that?"

Peter sat sullen. He had no choice but to explain what his sleeping arrangements had been since he was kicked out of his house.

"I was staying in the house while the owner was on vacation."

During this entire dialog, Sergeant Williams sat listening intently. Finally he broke his silence.

"I spoke to your boss. He said that you were staying at the old motel down the street from the post office, except for a night freezing in the parking lot."

"That is what I told him because I knew I would be fired if I told the truth," admitted Peter. "I had nowhere to live and no money to spend due to my pending divorce so I started to stay in houses that had asked the post office to hold their mail because they were going on vacation." Peter continued, "I know it was wrong but I was very careful not to touch their belongings. And I definitely did not steal anything. I just needed a place to sleep at night. I even brought my own sheets."

The officers looked at each other in disbelief.

"You brought your own sheets?"

"Yes and I took pictures of how to remake the bed so it would be just like the owner left it. I really tried to not disturb anything but the bed, though I did watch their TV." Peter kept looking at the men to get their reactions, but they were trained to control their nonverbal behaviors. Peter was not able to figure out what they were thinking, though he had to assume the worst.

"Do you realize this isn't the first robbery where we found your finger prints?" asked Sergeant Williams, from the back of the room, smoothing his salt and pepper hair back from his face.

"Yes," Said Peter nodding his head thoughtfully. "I guess you are talking about the house on Roosevelt. Yes, I was staying there until after work one day I saw masked intruders running out with the TV set from the bedroom." Then he added, "You must have found my wedding ring."

The officer quickly flipped through the pages on his clip board. "Frank Crawford's daughter did not mention seeing a wedding ring that wasn't supposed to be there. Why was it there?"

"I was staying there and my wife, or…soon to be ex-wife, was serving me papers of all different kinds and one night I took it off and put it on the bed stand." Peter looked at the Sergeant. "You should remember all of the papers that you served on me."

"Yes I do." Sergeant Williams added, "Are you aware of what else happened the night that house was robbed?"

"Yes," Said Peter thoughtfully. "After the thieves left I went in to see if I had forgotten anything and I saw a man lying on the floor unconscious."

"And you started CPR?" prompted the officer while waiting to see Peter's reaction.

"How did you…how did you know?" stammered Peter, turning pale this time.

"DNA," The officer said simply. "You left behind your DNA."

"Instinct told me to try to help him. But I couldn't get his heart going again. Believe it or not I'm a nice guy! But it was too late. His head was bleeding so I guess he fell or something."

"He was murdered you mean," The officer raised his voice. "And I think it was by you. Peter Johnson, you have the right to remain silent. Anything you say can and will be used against you in a court of law. You have the right to an attorney…"

"What? Peter panicked. "Are you arresting me? I didn't do anything!"

"If you cannot afford an attorney, one will be appointed for you."

"No!" Peter shouted, feeling his brains scramble almost like they shot him with the stun gun again. "No! I stayed there but I did not hurt anyone! I tried to help that man, not hurt him!"

"We are charging you with the premeditated murder of Frank Crawford." Sergeant Williams added solemnly. "We think you tried performing CPR because you suddenly grew a conscious and hoped he would live, but he didn't."

"Premeditated murder? Are you kidding me?" Peter was shouting in a high pitch thin voice now. "Are you kidding me?"

"No, we don't kid," Answered the officer. "Can you tell us how the back gate got oiled?"

"Well yes." Said Peter confused. "I oiled it because it was so noisy. I didn't want the neighbors to hear it when I went through it and be alarmed."

"Exactly," Finished the officer as he came over to put metal handcuffs on to Peter's wrists, "premeditation."

"How could it be that all three houses that have been robbed were listed in the post office as mail holds?   How could that be a coincidence?" The officer argued. "You are the obvious connection."

"Three houses?" Peter questioned the big stocky man. "The only other house I stayed at was on Stoney Point. Did it get robbed too?"

"Don't play coy with us. You know it was the house on Huston Drive." Said the officer frustrated. He grabbed Peter by the shoulder and started to lead him out of the room to put him in a waiting cell.

"I remember a house on Huston Drive was on the post office holds but I never stayed there." Peter was pleading to get them to listen to him now. "I only stayed at Stoney Point, Roosevelt and Emmet Street. I swear it! You have to believe me!"

"Hey!" He yelled trying to get them to listen to him. "I'm not the only person who does the holds at the post office. Everyone has access to them just by walking by. I just needed a place to stay! I did not kill anyone! I could never do something like that!"

"You need to get yourself a lawyer, or one can be appointed for you," the officer told him bluntly.

"I would," Peter said sadly, "If I could afford one. Or maybe I should say another one."

The officer kept hold of Peter's shoulder and pushed him ahead of him as they walked down the cold cement hallway. The big metal gates opened to let them through and then crashed together behind him. The sound of the grating metal made his skin crawl and his stomach grind like a blender full of onions. He had no idea how to get the officers to believe that he was only guilty of trespassing.

Peter thought about Pam and her little boy Drake. He wondered what they would think when he stopped coming to the park in the evenings, Ma too. He had made three good friends and now he would probably lose them. If only he could post bail but he once read that murder imposed a bail of more than one hundred thousand dollars. That was more than he ever had in his entire life, so he was sure he'd have to stay in jail.

Sergeant Williams stayed sitting in the chair in the interrogation room. He was deep in thought and tapped his forefinger against his cheek. He always felt he was a good judge of character. Somehow he couldn't see Peter as a murderer, even though all of the evidence pointed to him. The finger prints, the fact he was caught on the premise and the fact that he worked at the post office and had access to all of the hold information. He knew a court and jury would find Peter guilty easily with the evidence stacked against him. He couldn't understand why Peter would insist he stayed at a house other than those robbed.   He scratched the words 'Stoney Point' down on a notepad.

Sergeant Williams still had a nagging feeling that there was more to this story, and he knew it was up to him to prove it.

Chapter #19

Tell us every little detail

"Tell me every detail you can think of about both robberies. Don't leave anything out, even the smallest detail could mean something." Sergeant Williams was serious about helping Peter. Peter looked awful. Since he was put in jail last week he couldn't sleep or eat since he was so worried about his situation. He looked sickly, pale and thin. The scraggly beard and disheveled hair didn't help his appearance any either.

"I stayed in the house on Roosevelt for three nights but then the fourth night is when I came back and saw a shadowy figure in the yard. I watched for a few minutes while they loaded a white van up with things from the house and took off. There were three people involved, all wearing dark colors and face masks, like you wear snowmobiling in the cold weather. The van had a logo on its side door that was a buggy eyed mosquito. It was hard to miss."

Peter continued as Sergeant Williams made notes on a pad of lined paper. "Please check the van out. There can't be too many with that description in this city.   I know I should have called the police right then but I was afraid my trespassing would be discovered and I don't know how I would survive without my job. It's all I have left." Peter looked so desperate and sad. Sergeant Williams made no comment, but kept writing.

"When I got off work yesterday I went to eat at Ma's café. When I was walking out of the front door I saw the white mosquito van leaving the parking lot. I figured it had to be the same one so I got in my car and followed them. I couldn't believe it when they circled around the block three times, passing the house on Emmet Street and I realized they were casing it!"

Peter continued, "I saw them, there were three of them all dressed in dark clothes and ski masks again. I saw them park the van in the shadows across the street so I drove around the corner and watched them break in and carry out a bunch of electronics. I thought they were going to go back into the house for more but they suddenly jumped into the van and left before I could call the police. Then there you guys were! I wonder if they had a police scanner or something because they left just in time so you wouldn't see them."

Peter took a deep breath and continued with his voice sounding more and more like a whine. "Then I don't remember too much after that since it's hard to think after you've been stunned. It really scrambles your brains you know."

"Yes, but it's better than us shooting you." The Sergeant replied chuckling.

"No doubt about that, I guess." Peter said. "Though at the time, I felt like I had been shot."

"Can you think of anything else?" The Sergeant urged him to think. "Even a small detail, something that seemed out of place?"

The only other thing that I remember is, after you put me in the police car I sat and watched the parade of curious spectators. I saw a yellow mustang driven by Jenny, a girl that works at the post office and someone else was in the passenger seat, I'm assuming her boyfriend. I hate this girl with all of my guts…ugh…and I couldn't believe she would drive by when I'm experiencing my lowest low." Peter shook his head slowly. Just his luck, but hopefully she didn't see him. He was embarrassed enough already.

Chapter 20

Jail

Jail sucked. Peter sat on a cold cement bench all alone in his cell. The walls were scratched and worn from years of wear. The stainless steel toilet sitting beside his bed was as clean as he could make it but it still smelled like sewer gas. The sheets on the 'hard as a rock' cot were thread bare and rough. The pillow smelled like sweat and had to be folded in half to even start to be comfortable.

Since he was in jail for a charge of murder he found out quickly that he would get no respect from any of the guards or other inmates. Most other prisoners were allowed to spend time in the activity room, watching TV, playing pool or dealing cards. He was allowed access to a small radio, and an old newspaper everyone else got to read first.

Even just getting to do a cross word puzzle would have been a welcome distraction, but someone always completed it before it got to him. He started to try to entertain himself by counting letters in a random newspaper paragraph. He guessed it would contain 13 letter A's, then he would count to see if he was correct. It was pretty dull, but better than no stimulation at all.

This morning was his seventh day in jail. He was counting the letter H in a newspaper story and he was listening to the radio at the same time.

"This is Donna Reynolds reporting for KRCC TV. Two weeks ago, Frank Crawford was murdered in his home at 1705 Roosevelt. The police department has confirmed that they have a suspect in custody. His name is Peter Johnson. He has been charged with premeditated murder and robbery. They have also linked the suspect to robberies at Huston Drive, Emmet Street and at Roosevelt."

"We, the public, can all sleep more peacefully knowing that this suspect is behind bars. This is Donna Reynolds reporting for KRCC TV."

Peter sat with his head in his hands. Now everyone would know of his plight. He thought of the shock Pam would feel. She was probably horrified to think Drake had loved playing with his 'Peeta.'

And Ma! She had been so generous to him. She probably felt foolish and gullible that she had been so kind to a murderer. He was sure she regretted sending home all of the treats and goodies.

"Hey murderer!!" A large loud voice yelled from the cell next door. "It doesn't take much to kill an old man. Are you going to kill little kids next?   Be a man and at least try to kill someone your own size and age!"   The deep belly laughs that followed could be heard reverberating down the cell block. Several other inmates started to yell obscenities too. It grew louder and more menacing.

"I didn't do it!" Peter yelled at the top of his lungs. "I didn't kill anyone, old or young!"

"Sure buddy. We are all innocent too." The loud voice next door kept taunting him. "Didn't you get the memo? None of us should be in here!"   And again the laughter rose to a dull roar up and down the echoing cell block. Everyone was having a good laugh over Peter's situation.

"But I AM innocent!" He insisted. "I AM!"

The shrill whistle attacked his senses like having a glass of cold water thrown in his face.

"Lights are going off! For inciting a riot all privileges will be revoked until tomorrow morning. No radio and NO TALKING!" The guard strutted by swinging his billy club to show them he meant it. He was a big man who obviously spent many hours a week lifting weights. He had short hair resembling a military cut.

He stopped in front of Peter's cell and said, "And that means you! We had a nice calm group here before you joined us. If this kind of thing happens again, you will be put in solitary until you learn what is expected." He raised his club to make sure Peter understood that this was a threat. Only a real brave person, or a real stupid person, would want to go against that club powered by those pumped up muscles.

"I will be quiet." Peter looked apologetic. "It won't happen again."

The guard continued down the cell block in total silence. For a big man, he had a very agile body. For a moment Peter wondered if he had been a marine in a former life, but he knew it would be an idiotic thing to ask. Silence was safer.

No one wanted to challenge the menacing guard. He walked the entire block without a peep from anyone then tapped the metal doors at the end of the block with his club. The doors slid open and he disappeared behind them with a heavy metal clank.

"You'd better hope they keep you in that cell," said the deep voice from the neighboring prisoner as soon as the guard was out of ear shot. He continued with a voice just above a whisper. "I hate losing my privileges! If I get my hands on you, I promise you'll wish you were in solitary."

Peter swung his body onto his cot and pulled the sparse blanket over his head. He could only guess what his neighbor had in store for him.   None of those guesses were pleasant.

Chapter #21

The white van

"You have a visitor," said an older guard as he fumbled trying to open the cell door. He held a club in his hand and wore a big handgun on his belt. "Turn around. I need to cuff you."

Peter did exactly as he was told. That seemed to be the best way to survive in this place. He wondered who the visitor was though. He didn't think anyone really cared about him, especially enough to come to such a nasty place for a visit.

He shuffled down the hallway with the guard following close behind, billy club in hand, ready if needed. A metal barred gate opened up and the older guard gave him a nudge with his club to make him go through.

He entered into a small hallway lined with big metal doors. One door was open and the guard motioned for him to go in. "Sit down," Was all the guard said before closing and locking the heavy door behind him.

A large barred wall was in front of him and he sat in the stiff wooden chair provided.

A single light shined from the ceiling. A door on the other side swung open and in walked Jerry. He took a seat opposite Peter and smiled, "Hi."

"Jerry, it's not what you think." Peter frantically tried to explain. "I did not kill anyone! It's true that I stayed in those houses, and for that I am very sorry, but I never stole anything or hurt anyone. I was just so desperate!"

"Unfortunately, I have to suspend your benefits and your job until the court case is over. Of course you are considered innocent until proven guilty." It looked like Jerry was sincerely sorry to have to deliver this kind of news. "Either way, I doubt we'll be working together again."

Peter slumped down in the cold wooden chair. The fight had gone out of him.

"I know I screwed up but I did not kill anyone or rob anyone," He insisted. "It was the men in the white mosquito van. But I can't prove it and no one will believe me." He finished sadly with his head hanging down on his chest.

"What mosquito van?" Jerry asked confused.

"It is a white cargo style van with a decal on the door of a buggy eyed mosquito. I never saw any words, just the ugly bug. I first saw the van at the house on Roosevelt and then later on Emmet Street. I hid and watched them load the van full of things from the houses both times, but not on Huston Street. I never stayed at Huston Street!"

"Peter, I believe you." Jerry said sympathetically widening his eyes as big as he could. "I just can't imagine you doing anything to hurt anyone except maybe by having an extramarital affair. That I do believe you did."

"Yes I did." Peter shook his head. "I guess that discretion is something I will keep paying for...over and over."

When Jerry was driving home he kept thinking about their conversation. Peter had talked about a mosquito van. That struck a chord of familiarity. He thought he had seen a white van recently with a decal, but he couldn't remember exactly where.

Jerry hated the idea that his office had been used for criminal activity. He could never forgive Peter for staying at those houses, even though he understood his desperation. Everything that happened in that office was a reflection on him and the job he was doing managing it. Jerry still had four years until retirement and he wanted to keep his job in order to spend his old age with full benefits.

Suddenly Jerry slowed up and pulled into a parallel parking spot in front of a discount furniture store. He scooped up his cell phone from the leather passenger seat beside him. After a moment to locate the correct number, he dialed.

"Good afternoon, Martinsdale police department… Kristy speaking."

"Kristy, could I speak to Sergeant Williams?"

"Yes, just one moment. I'll connect you."

Chapter #22

1214 Westside Drive

Jerry's mother was seventy six years old and she was a snow bird. She lived in the Midwest during the summer but spent her winters in Phoenix just like migrating birds do, thus the name.

Jerry forwarded her mail to her every week after collecting it daily and taking it home with him. He had done this for several years to help her out. He now decided to put her address of 1214 Westside Drive on hold to make collecting her mail a lot easier. He would still mail it to her once each week. She owned a home in the neighborhood and Jerry, being the good son, was responsible to watch over it while she was gone for the winter.

He was setting up the hold box for his Mom while he was talking to Jeff, the new guy filling in for Peter. Jeff transferred in from the bulk mail center on a temporary assignment. A couple of the delivery route people were in the building too. They were in the back room but Jerry could hear their conversation plainly.

Jerry started to explain his Mom's situation to Jeff. "My Dad had a large gun collection. My mom has it now since he passed away. He had rifles, multiple handguns and even a musket that's a couple of hundred years old. Plus he had stored away enough ammo to support a small army!" Bragged Jerry loudly, laughing the whole time.

"My Mom doesn't want to part with any of them. She just stores them all in the basement in many large Rubbermaid containers to keep them dry from the damp conditions. The containers look like a series of colorful coffins all lined up in a row." Jerry paused with a chuckle then became more serious. "With all of these robberies going on I've decided to install a whole house alarm system but they can't put it in until this coming Friday. I'm glad I can get it installed before my Mom comes back from Phoenix."

"Guns like that are really worth some bucks!" Jeff said as he started to sort letters onto the hold shelves. "Doesn't it scare you to have your Mom sleeping there with all of that temptation?" Jeff wasn't too bright but he did follow directions very well. Jerry thought he could make a good substitute for Peter if necessary.

"No, 'Cause no one knows they are there. And no one expects an elderly lady to have a basement full of guns. So I'm not too worried."

"I suppose that is true. But I bet you'll rest better when you know your mom and the guns are better protected."

"Yes I will," Jerry responded. "I really will. I'm glad Friday morning is only two days away. Then I can relax."

Chapter #23

The angry neighbor

Whenever Peter left his cell he hurried back as quickly as he could. He started taking his meals in the cell too, but he couldn't shower in the cell. It was the day of his arraignment and he knew he would not look like a respectable citizen if he smelled like a men's locker room and had greasy hair.

"It's shower time," announced the muscle bound guard as he unlocked the door to let him out. " You need to 'pretty up' before going to court."

Peter hesitated but then asked, "Do you know where the guy in the cell next to me is now?"

"Why? Are you planning on causing us more problems today? Are you two planning a rendezvous in the shower?" The bulky guard grinned like he thoroughly enjoyed the thought.

"No…of course not. I…I was…just curious. He's a pretty scary guy."

"Well, he's not a murderer like you so you have nothing to worry about."   The guard looked closely at Peter. "I have to admit that you don't seem like any of the murderers I've had in here before. You're as scared as a rabbit. But I guess one never knows, since murderers come in all shapes and sizes."

"But I'm not a murderer!" Peter argued vehemently. "I just made a stupid mistake that snowballed on me. I'd never physically hurt anyone. Heck, I tried to give him CPR!"

"That's what they all say," and the guard stopped to open the door to a large shower room. Luckily no one else was in there.

Yet…

Chapter #24

Kristy

Sergeant Williams sat waiting, holding the phone to his ear and ready to respond to an answer.

"Hello?" A timid female voice asked.

"Is this Sheila Crawford?"

"Yes?"

"This is Sergeant Williams from the Martinsdale police force. Do you have time to answer a question for me?"

"Sure Sergeant, what can I do for you?" The female voice sounded more confident now.

"Sheila," asked the Sergeant. "Did you find a wedding ring in your father's house, maybe on the dresser, in the bedroom or on the floor? It is gold and has initials written inside of it."

"A wedding ring?" Sheila asked confused. "No, I can't imagine my Dad having a wedding ring other than the one he wore and I haven't found another one either. We have removed all of the furniture and his belongings from the house so I'm pretty sure we would have found it if it was there."

"Thank you very much." The Sergeant added, "Again, I am so sorry for your loss and we are doing everything we can to try to figure out what happened to your Dad."

"Thank you and let me know if I can help in any way." She hung up the phone wondering why a ring would be in her father's house and what that had to do with the investigation.

The Sergeant sat contemplating his next move. After a moment he reached for his cell phone, his coat and his hat. He walked out by the front desk where Kristy sat addressing some envelopes.

"Good morning Kristy," the sergeant said smiling wide.

"Good morning to you too!" answered Kristy, with a similar big smile.

"If anyone needs me I will be back right after I visit a couple of jewelry shops. And just so you know…that color really looks nice on you." The sergeant turned and walked out the front door, moving quickly and with purpose.

Kristy smiled. She had seen that walk before. She knew he was on to something.

Chapter #25

The shower

Peter really needed this hot shower. It seemed to clear his brain of his worries and his bones of his aches and pains. He threw his head back and scrubbed his hair with the unscented shampoo, using both hands. He started feeling more positive about the events ahead of him that day.

"Aargh!!!" He screamed and he ran out of the shower stall across the slippery wet cement floor, dancing like an Indian around a fire in an old fashion western.

"Ha Ha!" Deep voices laughed at him. "What? Didn't we make that bucket of water cold enough for you? We filled half of it with ice cubes but maybe you would have preferred hot water…boiling hot?" And the two men slapped hands at how funny they thought it had been.

"Leave me alone!" yelled Peter, grabbing a towel off of the hook and wrapping it around himself. He ran out of the shower room as fast as he could losing his footing and narrowly catching his balance in time to keep from crashing on the floor.

The two men followed him out the door and grabbed him by the towel, the force of which spun him around in a circle cascading him to the cold cement floor naked.

The tallest prisoner was his next door neighbor, verified by his deep voice, who had delighted in torturing him with verbal threats. His bald head was shiny and peppered with moles. The shorter one appeared to be his flunky and literally just did as he was told. His face was sagging down causing creases along his nose and the corners of his mouth. Peter doubted that even smiling would not take away the angry look on his face.

"Kick him!" yelled his neighbor in his low gruff voice.

The shorter man started to pummel Peter with kick after kick. Peter turned his back to the man to protect his face and more sensitive male areas. Each kick caused him to grunt out in pain.

"Stop it!   Stop it now!"   A loud commanding voice yelled out.

Both prisoners took off running the other direction down the hallway. "You will both be confined to your cell for four days for this!" The guard threatened them as they turned the corner at the end of the hallway, heading back to their cells.

"You'd better get back in the shower," the guard told Peter as he watched him try to stand up.

"Why back in the shower? I'm already clean," said Peter totally distraught and shaken.

"You have a head full of shampoo. I don't think that would impress the judges any today. I'll guard the door so you can wash it out." The guard followed him to the shower stall ignoring all of the scrapes and bruises starting to show on Peter's body.

"Thank you for helping me out." Peter said quickly rinsing his hair and rewrapping it in the wet towel.

"Don't mention it. And I really mean that…don't mention it to anyone." The guard smiled. "I don't want anyone to think I'm getting soft but like I said before, you sure do not seem like a murderer. If you are going to stay here you'll need to learn how to handle yourself. The way it is going now you won't last too long." The guard stayed with him until he got dressed, then followed him back to his cell.

. "Good luck today." And he tapped his billy club on the bars to signal the cell door to be closed. The other two prisoners were already in their cells.

A rolled up newspaper was being tapped against the bars of his cell and finally pushed through, landing on the floor in a flutter as it unrolled.

"Take it!" The low voice instructed angrily.

Peter wasn't going to take it but his neighbor got louder and more insistent. He reached down and hesitantly picked up the paper. He unrolled it the rest of the way and saw there was writing on it in big black smeary marker.

"You are in big trouble now. We won't be as nice next time," and to accentuate their meaning they added a picture of a stick figure hanging in a noose.

Peter took the pillow case off of his pillow and ran cold water on it. It felt good against the swelling bruises appearing on his arms and legs. Hopefully he would not be there too much longer.

Chapter #26

1723 Stoney Point

Sergeant Williams was checking addresses as he drove slowly down the street. Finally, 1723 Stoney Point was in front of him. He parallel parked the car along the side of the street, and hurried to the passenger side to help Jeremy, another detective, take out his fingerprint kit. They each carried one of the cases and they walked up the cement sidewalk to the house. They rang the doorbell and after a few moments they could hear someone slowly shuffling to the door and finally opening it.

"Hello," said a creaky voice belonging to a short elderly woman, peering through a crack in the door. "Who are you? What do you want?"

"Hello Ma'am. My name is Sergeant Williams." He opened up his badge for her to see and held it up to the narrow opening.

"I don't want you to be scared but I have reason to believe that someone entered your home a few weeks ago and I was wondering if you would allow us to come in and dust for fingerprints?"

Chapter #27

The arraignment

The ride to the courthouse for his arraignment was uneventful but Peter enjoyed every minute of it. How nice to be outside in the sun again and able to take a ride through familiar city streets. He sat in the back of a prison van, handcuffed and wearing leg irons. He was wearing a bright orange jump suit but his body and hair were clean and his spirits were high. He had never attended an arraignment before and was hopeful that somehow his nightmare may be over because of it. He was ready to explain his situation with his hand on a bible. Maybe someone would finally believe him.

He shuffled into the courtroom followed by an armed guard. The courtroom was very brightly lit and it was like falling asleep on the beach and opening your eyes directly into the sun. He blinked and squinted until he could finally see clearly. And in the front row, smiling weakly, he saw Pam.

He had not spoken to Pam since his arrest. His first reaction was to smile at her, but he soon followed that with embarrassment, total head to toe, pit of the stomach, embarrassment. He never imagined himself being in this awkward position. He wished he could go speak to her and tell her his entire story but in a way he was glad she was there so she could hear what *really* happened when he was allowed to testify.

Peter's court appointed lawyer, Jill, was sitting at the front table waiting for him. He had only met her one time, and wouldn't even have recognized her if they hadn't pointed her out to him. How was she going to defend him when she barely knew his story or anything about his character?

"Stand up, the judge is entering the court room," Jill said beneath her breath, nudging him with her elbow in his ribs. Peter struggled to his feet, finding it hard with the leg irons and handcuffs.

"ALL RISE! The district court of Polk County is now in session. The honorable Judge, Jake Simpson, presiding. Please be seated." The bailiff said with authority. You could tell he was wearing a bullet proof vest, along with a belt covered with all of the necessary police equipment and a handgun hung in a leather holster at his side.

"You can sit down now." Jill whispered to Peter.

The bailiff continued, "Your honor, today's case is Polk County vs. Peter Johnson. The charge is premeditated murder."

The judge looked at Peter with piercing eyes.   That few seconds of scrutiny seemed like many minutes, with Peter feeling the full intensity of the charge.

"Who is representing the defendant?" asked the judge, Jake Simpson.

"I am.   Jill Osmond, for the defense, your Honor."   And Jill stood up to meet Judge Simpson's stare. Peter had never met Jill before but he had been told an attorney had been appointed to him since he couldn't afford to hire a lawyer on his own. He looked over at Jill while she waited for the Judge's direction. She was very young, probably straight from taking her bar exam. She was very pretty and she seemed very confident in how she handled herself. He had no idea what to expect at this procedure so he had no choice but to trust her.

"How does the defendant plead?" Asked the judge routinely, now concentrating on the papers in front of him.

Jill looked at Peter and said, "Stand up…Say not guilty."

Peter stood back up to reply, "Not guilty, Sir, because I was only…"

"No discussion. Please sit down." The judge started to fumble around with papers on his desk, dismissing Peter completely.

"The plea has been entered. Your case will come to court on May 5th, at 8:00 a.m." and the Judge dropped his gavel firmly on the desk.

Suddenly everyone stood up with a scraping of chair legs on the cold tile floor and no one spoke a word. The judge stood and walked out of the courtroom through the door he entered from, with a flowing of black robes.

"What happened?" Peter whispered to Jill, concerned and confused. "I didn't get to tell my side of the story!"

"It's over. This was just an arraignment. We come back in May to present our case. I'll come to the prison to discuss the case with you next week." And Jill walked away after the guard approached Peter and said. "It's time to go."

Peter looked back at Pam who was sitting silently in the front row. She was looking directly at him but had no expression on her face. She was sitting stiffly on the wooden bench with her hands tightly clasped on her lap. She looked so out of place. This was definitely a situation where she didn't belong. But neither did Peter.

"Can I have two seconds to speak to a friend?" asked Peter hopefully.

"No…we have to go," Answered the guard as he grabbed Peter by the arm and led him toward the side door and the waiting van.

He looked back over his shoulder but Pam was walking out of the courtroom and all he saw was her back.

All of his hopes were dashed by his ignorance of the court procedures. And how was he to survive several more weeks in prison?

Chapter #28

Pam

It was hot in the attic.   Sergeant Williams sat by the little window so he could see the back yard clearly, but the window contained the old fashioned single pane glass and though it would have felt better to open it and let the wind blow right through the metal screen it might have been noticeable from the outside. The air conditioning was on in the house and the downstairs was very nice and cool, but there was not any duct work allowing flow to the dark attic.

He sat on a creaky old chair covered with at least a decade of powdery dust bunnies that seemed to hop up and attach themselves to the brushed denim of his uniform pants. It looked like it was going to be a long night. Surveillance jobs were tough shifts to pull but quite often they turned out to be the most exciting when you least expected it.

He brought along a zip lock bag filled with pretzel sticks, and he pulled it from his pocket. He personally loved salty snacks even though his doctor had warned him that his high blood pressure would suffer if he kept eating them. But he knew from experience that munching on something, especially something crunchy, always helped him pass the time.

Sergeant Williams had a solid screen that framed his cell phone so he could play games on it without worrying that the bluish light would be seen outside of the window. He came into the house hours ago by entering the back door which was purposely left unlocked, and the old lamp fixture above the door was turned off to help conceal him. He decided the attic was the best place for him to view the immediate area. He also had his radio on silent, but still handy in case he needed to call for backup. Hopefully no one had noticed him crossing the backyard in the shadows, tiptoeing through the wet grass and slipping inside the door, closing it softly but completely.

As he watched the minutes slowly tick by on his watch he realized that his hunch may have been wrong. It was peaceful and quiet, definitely not a crime scene. Though he knew he would be back the next day to try again. He still had a feeling about this house.

As Peter walked down the hallway he wondered who was at the prison to visit him. He thought it was probably his lawyer Jill Osmond. It had been several days already and she had yet to contact him to discuss his case. He was anxious to tell his story; he just hoped he would get the chance.

A jab in his ribs with a hard wooden billy club left him short on breath. It also let him know which cubicle to go to and he staggered in and dropped heavily into the chair provided.

When the door opened he was surprised to see a familiar face, a beautiful kind face. Pam's dark blonde hair was swept up into a neat bun at the nape of her neck. Her blue eyes looked sad as she met his gaze. She spoke quietly.

"Hello Peter."

"Pam...I am so embarrassed to have you see me here but I have wanted to tell you what happened." The words gushed out of Peter uncontrolled even though he had practiced them many late dark nights lying in his cell. "I didn't kill anyone! Please believe me! I did stay in those houses but I never stole anything!"

"I believe you Peter." Her tanned skin was beautiful and clear. How he would have liked to be able to brush her cheek with his hand and hold her in his arms. "I know you weren't capable of doing all of these terrible things. Did you say you stayed in those houses overnight?"

"Yes I did. I knew it was wrong but I had no money and sleeping in my car meant I walked around drowsy all day and I was afraid I would lose my job if I couldn't concentrate on my work." Peter leaned forward and placed his hands flat on the small counter in between them. "Thank you for coming. I so wanted to explain this all to you at the court house but they wouldn't let me."

"I wouldn't be here if I didn't believe you." She smiled that flirty smile and added, "Plus Drake misses you. And he's usually a real good judge of character."

"I miss him too." Peter said brushing his hair back with his hand, suddenly conscious of the fact that he hadn't been able to shower for a few days. How he must look to her.

"As soon as I get my name cleared I would like to see you at the park again. Visiting there with you and Drake made me realize that there is a lot more to life than what I had. And I promise you that I did not kill or rob anyone. I promise!"

"It's time to go," a gruff voice demanded of Peter from the outer hallway. "Now!"

"I've got to go. Thank you for coming."

"Now!"

"You have no idea how much this has meant to me!" Peter called back over his shoulder as he hurried out of the cubicle.

"Isn't that nice, you got a visit from a pretty lady," said the gruff voice.

Peter turned and looked up to see the big bald man who was his cell neighbor. Standing to his flank was his friend that had the perpetual angry face.

"What are you doing here?" Peter said starting to shake inside. "Where is the guard?"

"He's not here," the bald man answered grinning and showing off his badly stained teeth, probably from crack.

"We planned a little party for you and invited some guests." In response they held up their fists. Peter realized they were the guests so he figured he had nothing to lose. He clenched his hand tightly and let loose with all of the energy he could muster. To his amazement he struck the big man square in the gut and knocked him off balance and down to the ground.

The other man screamed and attacked back. Peter was hit right in the eye and a second blow to his chest. The room started to spin and down he went, out for the count. The flunky man helped the bald man up and they both attacked by kicking Peter as he lay on the floor crumpled up tightly in a ball like a new born baby.

"Stop! I've drawn my weapon! Stop!"
The guard had finally come back to get Peter.
"Down on the floor! All of you!!"

Several guards came running in from
the hallway. They each grabbed hold of one of
the prisoners and held on tight. Peter was still
unconscious, and it would probably be awhile
before he would think about fighting again.

Two hours later Peter slowly started to
wake up. First thing he was aware of was a
wet cloth lying across his face. He reached up
and pulled it off. His eyes opened but one of
them remained a narrow slit, swollen from hits
he had received earlier in the fight. He looked
around the dark room and tried to figure out
where he was. There were no lights on in the
cell except for a dim halo coming from the
hallway through the small opening in the
heavy metal door. The cell was very small and
quite cold. He was only covered with a thin
blanket.

The metal door was dead bolted in three
places and each bolt made a large clank when
it was slid to the open position. Peter tried to
sit up when he heard the door opening but was
greeted with a deep stab in his stomach where
the flunky had punched him. He curled up in
a fetal position again and waited to see what
was going to happen.

The door swung open with the guard's strong arm. He stepped aside and in came a small mousy looking man with a long white coat and a short gray mustache.

"Peter Johnson?" The man said reading from a small white card. "I'm Doctor Anderson. How do you feel?" He looked up and his glasses slipped down the narrow bridge of his nose. With his middle finger he pushed them back where they belonged.

"I feel like I was run over by a truck, a real big truck!" As Peter talked the Doctor started to check him over by pulling several items out of his small medical bag.

"What happened to me? I only remember those guys tricking me into leaving the visitor area?"

"This is what you get when you start a fight. That's also why you're in solitary. For a full week I think." The Doctor said now shining a bright light into Peter's badly bruised eye.

"Start a fight? No…no they started the fight, not me!"

"I saw the tape. You threw the first punch. It was all caught by the cameras in the visitor area. That's why you are in solitary and the other two guys are back in their cells." He seemed satisfied Peter would survive and started to put his stethoscope back in his bag.

"What? I'm the one being punished? I don't understand. I threw the first punch because I didn't think I had any choice but to try to defend myself especially since there were two of them and they threatened me first." The doctor started to put some triple antibiotic ointment on the side of Peter's face where he had road rash from skidding across the cement floor.

"Ouch!" Peter whined. "But actually I may be glad to be sent to solitary. Frankly I wasn't doing too well mixing with the general population." Peter decided that he would feel safer shut away by himself. Hopefully that meant no one could come bother him either.

Chapter #29

Jill Osmond

"You have company," stated the guard as the big metal locks clanked to the side, one by one, until the door was open. In the hall way stood Jill Osmond, wearing a crisp navy blue linen suit, a string of pearls and carrying a black brief case on her arm.

She smiled and walked in, already fumbling in her brief case for a paper clipped stack of papers.

"Hello Peter. I hope you are doing ok." She paused and studied his eye carefully. "That sure is some shiner you have, nice purple color. They explained to me that you started a fight at the visitor's area so you are now in solitary. I hate to tell you but your actions are not helping your case at all." She opened a glass case and slipped on a pair of tortoise shell framed glasses and continued. "But I did get the okay to offer you a plea bargain." She looked at him and flashed him a perfect teeth smile.

"A plea bargain," Peter asked confused. "Why? I didn't do anything."

"Do you realize that the charge against you is *premeditated* murder? Do you realize that could mean life in prison?" She looked him straight in the eye with disbelief. "…or even worse!"

"Well yes, I do realize that but I did not hurt that man! All I did was trespass."

"The plea I have been authorized to offer you is to reduce the charge of premeditated murder down to manslaughter since the coroner can't prove that it wasn't an accident that he hit his head on the cupboard." She paused then tried to convince him. "This is a good deal! You need to consider it! It may only have a sentence of ten to twelve years! This is huge opportunity compared to the possibility of life in prison!"

"But I didn't do ANYTHING!!" Peter said exasperated. "I did NOT hurt that man! I am only guilty of trespassing!"

"I think you should consider it. You never know how things will go in the court room. But if you decide to turn it down I will be there to defend you."

"I am definitely turning it down. I will not say I am guilty of something I did not do!" Peter flopped down on his cot at that point. He crossed his arms to show his defiance. There was no use continuing the conversation.

"Guard," Jill said loudly. "I am ready to leave." The guard came and unlocked the heavy metal door and ushered Jill out. "Peter, I'll talk to you soon. I respect your decision." And the metal door shut with the three familiar loud clangs.

After sitting in the hot attic the entire night the day before, Sergeant Williams came better prepared this time. He wore lightweight socks, short sleeves and brought a big thermos of ice water. He felt really strong that tonight would be the night. He already informed the patrol cars to stay near the neighborhood and be prepared to come ASAP when he gives the word. Now he sat quietly, playing spider solitaire on his phone, scanning the back yard carefully out of the window every minute or so. The moon was full tonight and definitely would help see any activity in the tree lined back yard.

Just when he was ready to win a game of solitaire he stopped to look out the window again. On the edge of the yard he saw movement. It looked like two figures and they were moving very cautiously, dodging from shadow to shadow. After watching them closely he could tell they were making their way toward the back door of the house. He looked out toward the street and could see a vehicle parked underneath a leafless tree that allowed the moonlight to reflect off the white paint. It was a van, a white van.

The Sergeant picked up his cell phone and called the station. He remembered that Peter thought they possibly had a police scanner since they seemed to know they needed to leave before the police could arrive. He called the officers in the two local patrol cars on their private cell phones.

"I have a 10-31 in progress at 1214 Westside Drive, approach with caution. It looks like two suspects and another one driving a white van parked along Second Avenue. Do not approach the suspects until we can catch them with stolen goods in their possession. They are just entering the back door at this time." Sergeant Williams looked out the window being careful so the moonlight wouldn't allow them to see his reflection on the glass. The two figures were cautiously entering the back door. He decided to stay on watch until someone left the house with stolen goods. He could hear subtle sounds from below and he realized they were going into the basement.

After what seemed like a very long time he saw a shadowy figure leave the back door carrying a large object in his arms. He retreated in the same manner that he arrived by darting from shadow to shadow until he reached the van. A third suspect came out of the driver's seat and opened up the back double doors of the vehicle so the object could be placed inside. Sergeant Williams now got a better look at the object. It looked like a colored tub that must be fairly heavy from the manner in which it was handled.

The Sergeant smiled. He loved it when a plan came together.

A second figure stepped out of the back door and made his way toward the white van. He also was carrying a plastic tub that appeared quite heavy. The first figure started to make his way back into the residence when bright flashing lights suddenly turned on from every side and a police car rushed in from each end of the street to block the van in its parking spot.

The officers quickly had the two suspects face down on the cement and were jerking their arms behind them. Zip strips were pulled tight and secure.

The last figure was just reaching the house so he slipped inside to hide. That is when Sergeant Williams made his entrance by surprising him with a loaded forty four held to the side of his head. He walked him outside and turned him over to the other officers.

After photographing the contents of the back of the van, one of the bulky plastic tubs was opened. The inside was filled with more than a dozen handguns. Luckily the criminals didn't know they were useless. They were all handguns that had been confiscated by the department over the years. All of them had a part or two damaged or missing on purpose to keep them from being able to fire. It was a great way to keep unregistered guns out of criminal hands. They also came in handy for sting operations like this.

The face masks were pulled off one at a time. The first two were well known by the police department from previous burglary arrests. The third suspect had started to cry. As they pulled the mask off of her head her long auburn pony tail dropped down her back. Her green eyes were wet with tears.

"You have the right to remain silent..."

Chapter #30

Jenny Swenson

Each suspect was stripped of their personal belongings and they were all collected in separate manila envelopes. The items would be matched with burglary reports to see if they would connect the suspects to other crimes. Finger prints were taken along with lots of vocal protesting. Mug shots were next, with only enough cooperation from the suspects to accomplish it. Three angry mug shots were the result.

The three suspects were then ushered into an interrogation room so the Sergeant could gather some initial information.

"What were you doing in the house on Westside tonight?"

"I don't know what you are talking about. I wasn't in that house," Sam, Jenny's boyfriend, argued confidently. "Roy, do you know what he is talking about?"

"No...I don't. I was just out taking a drive around the block. I wasn't in someone's house."

"Well then...why did you have two large bins full of handguns in the back of your van?" The officer demanded.

"I have no idea what you are talking about. I've never seen a bin full of handguns. What are you trying to pin on us?" said Sam who was definitely the smart aleck of the three.

"I have all of the proof I need to charge you with robbery tonight. What about the house on Huston Drive or the house on Emmet Street? Were you at these houses?"

Jenny finally quit sniffing and decided she had better start to fight for herself. "I have never been at any of those addresses except to deliver mail. I'm a mail carrier."

"Thank you Jenny, I'm glad you decided to join us. Now which of you killed the elderly man at 1705 Roosevelt?" If someone will confess I can promise a better deal to that person, but only to that person. Right now you are looking at premeditated murder which is a sentence of life in prison or an injection. Otherwise you will all be charged with the crime."

Jenny had started fake crying again. "We…I mean I…wasn't there! You can't just start accusing us of everything that has happened in this city!" She started to sob and tears ran down her cheeks. The Sergeant now saw his chance.

"Jenny, how old are you…about twenty eight or twenty nine? That means you could spend fifty to sixty years behind bars before you finally get out by dying. Is that the life you want? Think about it! Is that the life you wanted for yourself?"

"Nooo…it's not the life I want. But I didn't hurt that man. We were there but I didn't hurt that man!" She covered her eyes with the tissue.

"She's talking crazy!" said Sam quickly and loudly. "We weren't there! She doesn't know what she's talking about!"

"Yes I do Sam. I was there but I'm not getting charged with killing that man. I didn't do it!"

The Sergeant saw her weakening. "Then who did kill him Jenny…who?"

Jenny sniffed a few more times then suddenly became calm. "Our accomplice Peter Johnson did it. He killed the old man."

It was an answer that the Sergeant did not expect, not at all. He had not given Jenny enough credit for being cunning or he really was a bad judge of character when it came to Peter Johnson.

"Separate them to different rooms. Do not let them to talk to each other. Not even one word. Do it quickly."

As the three were ushered from the room by officers, amid threats of what would happen if they talked, the Sergeant started to open the manila envelopes.

The first one held a necklace, a pair of diamond stud earrings and a garnet ring. He assumed it was Jenny's items.

The second envelope held a brown well worn wallet containing twenty one dollars and a driver's license. It belonged to Roy along with a piece of spearmint gum and a couple of paper cough drop wrappers.

The last envelope held a set of car keys with a mustang emblem attached to them. Then there were a few folded up Kleenexes and a simple wide gold band. The Sergeant picked up the ring and examined it. He noticed it looked like something was inscribed inside. He squinted and finally could read the initials BJ+PJ.   Sam's last name was Lawsen so it seemed unlikely that it belonged to him. He would definitely have the detectives compare the ring to the lists of items stolen from the various houses.

Chapter #31

Roy Myers

"So Roy…I see in your record that you have been arrested for theft in the past.   You also did some time for it."

"So what about it?" Roy said boldly. "I did my time.   I paid my debt to society as you cops say. That's no reason for you to assume I did something wrong. You can't hold my past against me."

Roy sat at a metal table in a small brightly lit white walled room. One wall was covered by a large mirror. Everyone knew these mirrors were usually two-way with a few cops standing watching on the other side. Though tonight they were short staffed so only a camera was recording the conversation.

"That is true but we caught you red handed tonight. I also know I can connect you to the burglaries at Huston, Emmet and to the robbery and murder at Roosevelt."

"Jenny is crazy!   Just because she says *she* was there has nothing to do with me. Absolutely nothing!" He showed his disgust by spitting on the floor beside his chair. Now it was the Sergeants turn to be disgusted.

"Who killed the man at Roosevelt?" Sergeant Williams flipped a couple of pages on his clip board for effect. "I can make you a deal if you tell me. Do you really want to be sent up for life if you didn't do it?"

"I didn't do it.   Like Jenny said our friend Peter did it.   He was in on the robbery and he killed him. He pushed him right into the cupboard and he was bleeding all over the place.   I had nothing to do with it." He sat back in his chair with his hands folded over his stomach. He smiled a smile that said 'I think I'm winning.'

"How do you know he was pushed into a cupboard?   That information was never released. How do you know that?"

Roy looked panicked for a moment and his eyes opened wide. "I'm done talking without a lawyer here" he hissed through his clenched teeth, and he leaned back and closed his eyes to show he meant it.

"I'm done. You had your chance, too bad for you." Sergeant Williams said "Keep him in here," to the officer outside the door as he left and headed to the next room.

Chapter #32

Sam Lawsen

"Sam...Is that short for Samuel?"

"No, it's short for Sam," he said as he taunted the officer. "What's your name short for? A-hole?" He started to laugh thinking he was real clever.

"You can call me Sir." Sergeant Williams said as he settled himself into the second interrogation room. "Thanks to Jenny I got a confession implicating you to the robbery and murder at Roosevelt. But it wasn't necessary because Roy sang like a preschooler yelling out the words to wheels on the bus." He chuckled, "Have you heard that one? They go round and round."

"I've heard it. But you will never convince me that Roy squealed. He's not that type. He's a brick wall."

"So you think. Tell me about him?"

"No...You have the wrong guys. Peter killed the guy. He told me about it. We really don't even know Jenny so why would we be in some house with her?" Sam looked him straight in the eye as he spoke. He was good at this game.

"What's Peter's last name so I can go find him?"

"I…um…I don't remember. I was probably drinking when I talked to him so I don't remember."

"What does he look like? Give me a description then?" The Sergeant asked while writing on the side of his papers to record Frank's answers.

"I don't know…he's just a regular slob who robs houses and kills people. He's just average."

"Is he of average height, average build and average looks?"

"Yeah…he is average everything."

The Sergeant suddenly thought of a plan, pushed his chair back causing it to make a screeching sound as it scraped the floor and got up abruptly and headed for the door.

"Hey!!" Sam yelled after him. "What about me? Can I leave?"

The Sergeant didn't answer him. He just told the officer at the door that all three of the suspects cannot see or talk to each other. Plus they absolutely cannot watch TV or listen to the radio. He walked briskly out the door. He had a plan.

Solitary

Peter had not been out of his solitary cell for a few days and he was not complaining. He felt very safe where he was and his wounds were starting to heal. His lawyer Jill Osmund had visited the day before and he was starting to have some confidence that she could represent him at the trial. He also believed that she felt he was innocent and that was very important to him.

"Time to visit the Doctor," said a voice at the door while the locks were being slid over with the now familiar 'clang'.

When the door opened a single guard stood waiting. "Come on, what are you waiting for?"

"You mean I have to leave the cell? Can't the Doctor come to me instead?" Peter started to shake inside. His guts suddenly felt like they were being squeezed and he was afraid he would throw up. "I'm fine. I don't need to see the Doctor."

"That's not what my orders are. You need to get up off of that bed and come with me." The guard held up his billy club to show he meant business. And the look on his face told Peter the guard may even enjoy it if he resisted.

Slowly Peter went to the door as ordered, but not without looking both ways in the hallway before stumbling out the door.

"Your eye is looking good," said the doctor putting his lighted scope back on its holder on the wall. "You'll make a complete recovery with no loss of vision." The Doctor looked tired as he spoke. "Did I understand correctly that you are heading back to general population?"

"NO! I want to go back to solitary! Please!" Peter pleaded with real fear in his eyes. "Please don't make me go back to my old cell!"

"You'll be fine as long as you quit stirring up trouble. No one ever wants to stay in solitary.   Just quit fighting and egging on the other prisoners. You'll be fine." And he put his stethoscope back in his bag and walked out of the room, closing the door, leaving Peter there.

At first Peter expected a guard to come right in, but no one showed up. Finally the door knob started to turn. The door creaked open and a face peeked around the door with a wild grin. It was his neighbor from the cell block. Instinctively Peter stepped back behind the exam table to put some distance between them.

"Are you afraid…you should be. You definitely should be." The prisoner slowly moved toward Peter having only the exam table between them. Peter knew he couldn't defend himself until attacked, since that landed him in trouble last time. He looked up to the ceiling and saw a camera in the corner recording every detail so he just kept pushing the exam table around trying to keep it between them. Peter had an advantage being so tall because his arms were very long and he could control the table easier than his attacker. The prisoner reached out over the top of the table with both arms to grab Peter's shirt but Peter gave the table a hard thrust forward and hit him firmly in the gut, knocking the air out of the man.

Peter saw his chance and ran for the door and the hallway beyond. A guard lay on the floor where he had been knocked out giving access to Peter's room in the infirmary.

"Help me! Help me!" He yelled as he headed down the hallway afraid the prisoner would be right behind him. He threw open the door at the end of the hall to two shotguns pointing at his chest.

"Lay down, Hands behind your back!" The guard said, "Or we will shoot!"

"No, no! Don't shoot!" And he got down on the floor as fast as possible, following the orders to a T. His wrists were bound with the stiff zip ties and he was pulled up to his feet and escorted roughly out the door back toward solitary.

Thank goodness!

Chapter #34

Sergeant Williams

Peter was ushered out of the prison to a waiting van and was told they were going for a ride.

"Where are you taking me? Where?"

"A Sergeant Williams has requested your presence at the police station. Didn't you receive your engraved invitation?" the guard said it haughtily with a fake British accent. "Maybe they are inviting you to tea." The guard ended with a hearty chuckle thinking he was so amusing. The second officer joined in laughing.

Peter realized he was not getting anywhere so he just sat back with his hands still zip tied together and looked at the scenery as it went past. The trees were so green this time of year. How long had it been since he had spent a carefree evening at the park with Pam and Drake? It seemed like a lifetime ago.

When they reached the back of the police station they took him out of the car and directed him to go up a stairway to the back service door. The door opened and he was relieved to see Sergeant Williams waiting there.

"How are you Peter?"

"I'll feel better when someone tells me what is happening." Peter stated as the officer cut off the zip ties from his wrists.

"Don't worry. Do exactly as we tell you. We may have found a break in your case." Sergeant Williams was excited to see if his hunch was correct. Sometimes you could set people up and it would all fall apart. For Peter's sake he hoped this wasn't one of those times.

Peter was ushered into a room with extremely bright lights shining directly into his face.   Five other men were standing there, all wearing orange prison uniforms exactly like Peter's, but Peter didn't recognize any of them.

"I need everyone to line up facing forward. You all have been chosen for this lineup because of similarities in appearance to our suspect."   Sergeant Williams directed the group.

"What if I get picked?" asked one man jokingly. "Are you going to take my badge away Serg?" The man laughed at his joke though the Sergeant didn't seem to think it was very funny.

"As police officers you've seen this done hundreds of times. I need you to be serious and act the part. Joe, did you get finger printed?"

"Yes," said Joe as he held his hands up and looked at his ink stained fingers. "It's gross."

"Well just make sure you hold your hands so that your inked fingers show forward. "

"Will do, Sergeant."

Peter still wasn't sure what was going on but he realized these men were officers and it was a sting operation of sorts. He assumed he was just another guy to fill in the line. He realized at six foot four he rather stood out from the group since the closest man in height was only six or six one. He had come to trust the Sergeant so he decided it was best to just do as he was told.

Jenny came into the observation room alone. She had been sequestered from everyone all afternoon. She was sitting in a room by herself and the only thing to keep her busy was worrying. She was worn down to a frazzle and had lost most of her strength when it came to fighting her situation.

"Stand on the red line. Look through the window at the men and tell me which one is Peter." Jenny looked over and within a few seconds she said. "He's number four."

"Thank you.   Take her back to the interrogation room. Again, she speaks to no one."

Next Roy is ushered in with his hands zip tied and a confident look on his face.

"Stand on the red line. Look through the window at the men and tell me which one is Peter."

Roy's confident look faded very quickly. He concentrated on the six men in front of him. He decided the first one was too heavy considering you usually lose a lot of weight when you are first incarcerated so he deducted he wasn't Peter. He noticed that number three looked somewhat familiar.   Betting on the chance that he maybe had seen Peter at the post office in passing he decided to choose number three. Then he noticed number three also had ink on his fingers.

"I repeat, which one is Peter your accomplice?"

Because of looking familiar and because of the ink Roy said, "Number three."

Sam did not know where they were taking him but he knew his only chance was to keep accusing Peter. He hoped it would keep him from being charged with murder. So he spent the afternoon making up stories of how Peter planned all of the capers they had been involved in, anyway the ones the police had proof of. He knew he would get a robbery charge but defraying the murder charge to this Peter person was a brilliant idea of Jenny's. Sometimes he just didn't give his girlfriend enough credit for having beauty *and* brains.

The officer led him into a small darkened room.

"Stand on the red line." Through a glass window a bright light went on. He could now see six men lined up in a row in the next room. Sam had never been on this side of the two way mirror before, and immediately he knew he did not like it.

"Look through the window at the men and tell me which one is Peter, your accomplice."

Sam quickly looked the men over. None of them were familiar at all. Maybe it was a trick. Maybe none of them were Peter.

"I repeat, which one is your accomplice Peter."

"None of them, none of them is Peter. You are trying to trick me you SOB!" Sam started to head for the door to leave. He was instantly grabbed by two officers and was taken back to his sequestered room.

"Book them, all three for robbery and suspected premeditated murder. We have sufficient evidence to hold them." Sergeant

Williams stated. But he knew it would still be a long process before anyone would be found guilty of the murder. The wheels of justice turn so slowly. But today the Sergeant felt he had scored.

Sergeant Williams watched the video tape of the lineup. From it he could produce evidence that Jenny was the only person who knew who Peter was due to working together at the post office. The testimony from the two guys that repeatedly stated that Peter was their leader and planned all of the robberies would be hopefully thrown out in court. They both described many burglary planning meetings so it seems logical that they would have been able to identify Peter. The Sergeant had to laugh though at Roy. Officer number three was chosen on purpose since they hoped he would look familiar. But Roy didn't catch that he looked familiar because that officer had arrested Roy two months previous! Too funny! Sometimes it worked!

Chapter #35

The trial

"ALL RISE," yelled the bailiff to the crowd in the court room. "The Honorable Judge Jake Simpson is now entering the court room." The bailiff in this courtroom was actually a US Marshall, complete with a uniform of army green pants, a tan shirt stiffly starched, and a dark brown tie with a gold tie clip. His black belt held everything he may need to do his job which was maintaining order in the courtroom, including a large handgun and a taser which Peter would rather forget he was familiar with.

A short stuffy looking man stood in the doorway to his chambers. He walked in to the courtroom with his black robes flowing around his very shiny black shoes. He stepped up behind the bench and seated himself with an array of authority.

Peter and his attorney were already seated at a table in front of the bar, which was the little wall or fence that separated the judge and attorneys from the audience. His attorney Jill Osmund explained the workings of the courtroom in advance so he might feel more comfortable at how it works. When he was in court for the hearing he really didn't know what was going on so he was thankful she took the time to explain it all to him. It did help.

Peter found it interesting that back in history a bar was erected across the courtroom to keep the audience from rushing up to the judge, attorneys or prisoner. No one was allowed in front of the bar, except for the prisoner, that had not passed the exam giving you license to become an attorney. Which led to the exam being called the 'bar' exam and it was referred to as 'passing the bar' as passing the test to now give you permission to stand in *front* of the bar instead of staying back with the audience.

Jill also explained the witness stand used to be a place where the witness was forced to stand while giving testimony. Since sometimes a witness had difficulties standing a chair has been provided in more recent history, but the name has stayed the same.

"Good morning ladies and gentlemen. Now hearing the case of the People of the State of Missouri vs. Peter Johnson. Are both sides ready to present their cases?"

The District Attorney, an older man with a bad comb over, replied "Ready for the prosecution, Your Honor."

Jill Osmund stood up quickly and said, "Ready for the defense, Your Honor."

"Bailiff, has the jury been sworn in?"

"Yes they have, Your Honor."

"Thank you. Prosecution, you may call your first witness."

Peter looked over at the jury of people. None of them looked very happy to be here. They were probably hoping that they would not get chosen to serve. They looked like regular ordinary people. Hopefully they are not in a rush to go home because he needed them to try to understand his situation.

Peter also looked behind him. In the audience he saw Betsy. He was surprised to see her though he figured she was just curious about his situation.

Then he saw Ma. She smiled an encouraging smile to him. Ma…she was always the best.

Then he saw Pam. She was sitting next to Ma. She raised her hand as a small sign of hello. He couldn't believe she would still be supportive even though she really didn't know him that well. He so wished he could return to the park, relax comfortably on the wooden bench and explain his situation to her. If he hadn't stayed at the houses, this would have never happened.

"The Prosecution calls Jenny Swenson to the stand."

A door opened on the side of the room and in walked Jenny, followed closely by an officer. Her auburn hair was now worn long and loose, and clashed with her bright orange jail jumpsuit. Sergeant Williams had convinced the judge at the bail hearings that all three suspects needed to stay in jail and be kept from conversing with each other if possible to serve justice. Because of their charges of premeditated murder their bails were set at one hundred thousand dollars each. None of them could afford to pay that sum so in jail they remained.

But the Sergeant could not keep visitors from passing information from one to the other so he assumed their stories could be much more similar now. Either way, he had their initial testimonies, which were very different from one another.

Jenny stepped into the witness stand and gingerly took a seat. The prosecuting attorney approached her.

"Can you please tell me where you were on the evening of September 14th of this year."

"I...I was arrested that night." Jenny reached up and played with her long hair in nervousness.

"What were you arrested for?"

"Robbery."

"Then why are you being held in jail for premeditated murder?"

"Because the organizer of our burglaries, Peter Johnson, committed murder and I am being unfairly held for his crime, you know…guilt by association."

"You are lying!!!!" Peter jumped to his feet. "I did not organize burglaries! I did not kill that man!"

"Order in the court! Order!" yelled the Judge. He pounded his gavel on the desk several times.

"Please sit down. It is not your turn to speak," ordered the Bailiff as he rushed over to Peter to regain control.

"But she's lying!" Said Peter to Jill as he sat back down.

"It doesn't matter." She said putting a hand on his shoulder firmly as if she thought she needed to hold him in place.

"Sit down and be quiet. We will get our turn." Then to the Judge she stood and said, "I apologize, Your Honor. My client did not understand the rules. I guarantee he will not interrupt these proceedings again." As she said it she looked at Peter and gave him a stern warning look.

"I hope not," stated the Judge. "Or I may need to find him in contempt."

Peter sat quietly while Jenny explained how Peter was the mastermind of the robberies. Lie after lie flowed from her mouth. Peter sat staring at her as she spoke. How could he have ever been attracted to someone who could lie so easily. He immediately vowed to clean up his own life since he had to confess he was not much different in some ways.

Now it was Jill's turn to cross examine Jenny. She asked many questions designed to trip up Jenny, but Jenny held fast to her lies. She'd had a couple of weeks to sit in a cell to practice them and she had learned them well. Peter was starting to think he was caught in a sticky web he wasn't sure he could free himself from.

"The Prosecution calls Sheila Crawford to the stand."

Sheila walked timidly to the front of the courtroom. She took a seat in the witness stand and the prosecutor approached her.

"Ms. Crawford, first let me tell you how sorry we all are about the death of your father, Frank Crawford. I'm sure you miss him a great deal."

"Thank you. And yes I do, very much so. "

"Tell me what you discovered about your father's back gate?"

"Someone had oiled it."

"Why would someone oil a rusty gate in your Dad's backyard?"

"I guess I'm not sure unless someone wanted it to open without screeching like it normally did."

Jill stood up quickly. "I object. The prosecution is leading the witness and asking her to draw a conclusion instead of giving facts."

"I will withdraw the question," the prosecutor said with a sly smile. "I will rephrase my question. Did your father oil the gate?"

"Never," Sheila said with certainty." He did not like putting chemicals of any kind in the yard, so I know he did not do it."

"Thank you. That is all for this witness."

Jill stood up and smoothed down her pencil skirt before starting to speak.

"Is it possible that one of the other accused could have oiled the gate being careful not to leave finger prints?"

"Yes…I suppose so."

"Did your father have a gold ring that may have been stolen during the robbery?"

Confused Sheila answered, "No, I've never known him to have a gold ring other than his wedding ring. But his wedding ring was silver."

"Thank you. No more further questions."

"Ms Crawford, you may step down," said the judge quietly.

The Prosecution called Roy to the stand. His testimony mirrored Jenny's, at sometimes almost word for word. Then it was Jill's turn to cross examine.

"What is your profession Mr. Myers?"

"I'm a truck driver."

"Who do you currently work for?"

"I don't." Roy looked calm and composed but the fact that he kept wringing his hands told otherwise.

"Excuse me?   Did you say you don't work right now?"

"That's right. I don't"

"Why is that Mr. Myers?"

"I was let go, but it was okay since I wanted to find a better job anyhow."

"So…you were fired?"

"I guess you could call it that."

"Why were you fired?"

"My boss had it in for me. He never liked me from day one."

Jill picked up some papers from off of the table and started to flip through them. "Don't you mean you were fired for stealing merchandise from out of your truck and to escape prosecution you quit instead?" Jill stood right in front of him and demanded an answer.

"Hey, I wasn't arrested or anything."

"Maybe not but your boss, Mr. Jameson, is ready to testify that he caught you red handed with the merchandise and decided not to prosecute you because you returned the goods."

"This witness is not on trial here," interjected the prosecutor. "This witness's prior job is irrelevant to these proceedings."

"But it is vital to motive. I am trying to establish a motive." Jill Osmund pleaded. "A motive that is central to our defense."

"Sustain," the Judge replied, so Jill had to change her line of questioning.

"Why couldn't you pick Peter Johnson out of a lineup if you had worked so closely with him during all of these robberies?"

"I don't know…I guess he lost weight in jail or something so he looked different…but he killed the old man! I saw him do it!"

"That wasn't my question…If you saw him do it you should know what he looks like. You say you worked with Peter Johnson on multiple jobs and you say he orchestrated all of these robberies, so why couldn't you pick him out of a lineup?"

"I plead the fifth."

"So you refuse to answer on the grounds it may incriminate you?"

"Whatever you say…sure…yeah." Roy shrugged his shoulders for emphasis.

"Thank you. Would the court reporter please record the witnesses desire to plead the fifth. The witness can be excused."

"The Prosecution calls Sam Lawsen to the stand." Sam was being held in a side room and appeared in a few moments with an officer following him to the witness stand.

"Is your name Sam Lawsen?" started the prosecutor. The tall skinny man consulted a small notebook as he spoke.

"Yes it is."

"What were you doing on the night of September 14th of this year."

"I was arrested for robbery."

"Did you do it?"

"I guess there is no reason to lie at this point."

"Where were you on the evening of August 8th of this year?"

"I was apparently robbing a house on Roosevelt street."

"Did you get caught?"

"No."

"So getting caught at the house with all of the guns stored in the basement where you were arrested was not your first time committing robbery?"

"You tell me."

"In fact you have been arrested for burglary six times in your life?"

"Whatever you say."

"But in all of these robberies have you ever hurt anyone?"

"No…never."

"So what happened the night of the first? Why was this night different?"

"Peter killed a guy."

"Are you talking about the defendant Peter Johnson?"

"Yes. Peter was the brains behind us. He worked at the post office so he knew which houses were vacant. He would plan the burglaries and all I did was to 'do what I was told.' But he got out of control and killed the old man."

"How did it happen?"

"No one was supposed to be home but then this old man shows up. Peter tried to leave but the old man grabbed him and their legs got twisted together. Peter threw him up against a cupboard and I guess he hit his head. It was really bleeding."

"We apologize to Ms. Crawford for having to hear these details. I am done with this witness. The Prosecution rests."

Jill Osmund stood up and never took her eyes off of Sam's face.

"So Peter was 'the brains' of the operation so you say. But you were not able to identify him in a lineup. You thought we pulled a trick on you and Peter wasn't even in the lineup. But in actuality he was. Can you explain this?"

"Police are always playing tricks on me…and pulling my chain so I thought it was just another joke. If I would have looked closer I'm sure I would have picked him out." Sam sat back in his chair with his arms crossed over his chest. "But I didn't think it was all that important."

"Interesting that you didn't feel it was important," Jill said with amusement.

"What was Jenny Swenson's job during the robberies?"

"Sometimes she was the driver of the van, sometimes she helped carry things out of the houses."

"Houses? There must have been more than these two then. She also worked at the post office and had access to the same information that Peter had. Is this true?"

"I suppose. I really don't know what she did. I don't really know her very well."

"Oh… well we have surveillance tapes from the post office showing you met with her almost every day. So obviously you knew what she did. But in your initial interview you said you didn't know her at all. Why is that?"

"I guess I was trying to get out of being arrested."

"So you lied to the officers? How do I know if you are telling the truth now when you say you know Peter? I can prove you know Jenny from the tapes but I have no proof of you and Peter ever being together. Why is that?"

"I don't know. Maybe he knew the cameras were there so he never came out."

"So why couldn't you identify Peter the day the police brought you in for a lineup? You had already confessed your part and totally implicated Peter in the robberies and in murder. Why not go ahead and pick him out of a line up? You had nothing to lose and a lot to gain by pinning this murder rap on him. Why didn't you do it?"

"I...don't...know." Sam spat out each word as if they were distasteful. He was visibly shaken and little drops of sweat were forming on his forehead as he spoke. He nervously picked at his finger nails as he answered questions.

Jill opened a manila envelope that was lying on the table. "Do you recognize this?" She said as she held the simple gold band up for Sam to see.

"Hey, that's my ring. They took it off of me when I was arrested."

"It's nice. What initials are engraved inside of it?" Jill said as she squinted to see the tiny print inside the band.

"Initials? Don't trick me...there's nothing engraved inside."

"Actually there is. What do the initials stand for?"

Sam was sweating profusely now. He reached up and wiped the droplets off of his nose as they dripped down.

"I guess I didn't realize there were initials in there." Sam said as he wiped more sweat off of his temples. "But I have real bad eyesight so I probably just never knew they were there." Sam looked smug thinking he had cleverly avoided the trap.

"Where did you get this ring?"

"I don't know." Sam continued. "You see it was a gift from a girl friend."

"Was it from Jenny?"

"No…it was from a previous girl friend."

"What was her name?"

"I don't really remember…It was a long time ago."

"Surely you remember someone who gave you such an expensive ring." Jill pressed him. "What was her name?"

"Kathy…okay? It was Kathy."

"Does Kathy have a last name?"

"I don't remember."

"Either way her initials start with a 'K'. And yours would be 'SL'."

"I guess so."

"Thank you very much." Jill said to the Judge, "No further questions. I would like to call my last witness."

Chapter #36

Testimony

"The Prosecution calls Sergeant Williams to the stand." The Bailiff said in his loud booming voice.

When Sergeant Williams took his seat behind the witness stand the bailiff came forward to administer the oath.

"Do you promise to tell the whole truth and nothing but the truth so help you god?"

Sergeant Williams replied simply, "I do."

The prosecuting attorney approached the Sergeant. He was a tall skinny man that looked so serious, if he smiled his face may crack.

"Where were you on the night of September 14th of this year?" He said matter of fact.

"I was sitting in a stakeout at 1214 Westside Drive. I arrived at four o'clock in the afternoon." The Sergeant was very experienced at being a witness but he still found it nerve racking. Every detail needed to be exact.

"Why did you think this house was a good location for a stakeout?"

"Jerry Posia, the manager of the main post office, came to me with a hunch that it may be a target for a burglary."

The prosecuting attorney paused then asked, "Why did he think this house would be a target?"

"It was his Mother's home. He knew there may have been a connection between the post office and these burglaries so he was willing to work in conjunction with our office to plan a sting operation to test his theory."

"How did he pass on the information?"

"Jerry Posia waited until most of the postal employees were in the building and in casual conversation he confessed that his Mother, who was out of town, had a lot of guns in her basement plus a good deal of ammo." The Sergeant cleared his throat for a second. "He told them he was putting in an alarm system in her house in two days. He said he was doing this because he was worried since they were so valuable. He told them this to try to get the thieves to act quickly so we could set up a sting operation immediately. He also hoped none of his employees were involved, but he needed to find out."

"Did she really have a large amount of guns in her basement?"

"No…The police department provided the guns. They were all seized weapons from previous arrests, and parts had been removed to render them virtually useless." The Sergeant continued rubbing the stubble forming on his chin. "But the arrested individuals did not know that."

"So Mr. Posia lied to the postal workers?"

"Yes, he did."

"Mr. Posia was aware his former employee, Peter Johnson, was in jail for trespassing in houses based on information Peter gathered during his job at the post office. Mr. Peter Johnson was already in jail for stealing and for murder. Why did he feel the need to tempt the rest of the employees knowing this?"

"He wanted to make sure to test his employees to see if any more may be corrupt."

"So what happened on September 14th of this year?"

"We set up a sting operation and three individuals were apprehended at the scene in possession of stolen merchandise."

"And was there any involvement from Peter Johnson, the defendant, when it comes to robbing the property at 1214 Westside Drive?"

"No…he was in solitary confinement at that time and had no way to communicate with the three individuals who were arrested that night."

"No further questions for this witness."

Jill Osmund approached the Sergeant.

"What did Sam Lawsen, Jenny Swenson and Roy Myers say about Peter Johnson?"

"They said he was the mastermind of the burglaries. They said he committed the murder of Frank Crawford."

"Why don't you believe their testimony?

"Because except for Jenny Swenson, who worked directly with Mr. Johnson for several years at the post office, they could not identify Mr. Johnson in a line up. So it is hard to believe that they committed all of these burglaries together without being able to identify him."

"How did they describe him?" Jill asked quietly.

"Mr. Lawsen and Mr. Myers both said he was of average height, average build and of average looks."

"Why isn't that a good description? A lot of people are average." She probed for more detail.

"With your permission, Your Honor," The Sergeant said to the Judge. "Could I please ask Mr. Johnson to stand up?"

The Judge responded. "The defendant is requested to rise."

Peter stood up, all six foot four inches of him. He stood and looked around at the Judge and the audience.

The Judge requested, "The defendant may be seated."

"Would you say the defendant is average in height Sergeant Williams?" stated Jill Osmund.

"We only have one or two people on our entire police force that come anywhere near as tall as he is. No…I do not consider him to be average."   Sergeant Williams waited patiently.

"Do you feel that Mr. Johnson committed the murder of Frank Lawsen?"

Sergeant Williams looked over to Sheila Crawford apologetically. "I do not. After Frank Lawsen was assaulted Peter Johnson tried to revive him with CPR. We know this to be true because his DNA was present on the victim's lips. I have never investigated a case where the murderer actually tried to revive the victim. This would be a first."

"Why didn't he go to the authorities?"

"Due to his CPR training he knew the victim had passed and when he heard the rescue unit coming he decided to leave in order to hide the secret that he was trespassing in people's houses. He knew what he did was illegal but in my opinion I do not believe he committed the murder."

"What do you know about the ring that has   been   in   question   during   these proceedings?"   Jill held up the ring marked exhibit B.

"Sam Lawsen was wearing this ring when he was arrested and it was removed and placed with his personal belongings. According to his previous testimony he stated it was given to him by a girl friend named Kathy.   The ring has the inscription inside stating BJ + PJ.   After visiting a few jewelry stores I found *the* jeweler that engraved those initials for a couple whose names are Betsy Johnson and Peter Johnson.   Mr. Johnson reported back in August that he left the ring in the house occupied by Frank Crawford. This house was robbed that evening."

"Why was Peter Johnson in the home if he wasn't in on the murder and robbery?"

"He is going through a messy divorce and had no money to spend on a hotel room or apartment.   He states that he was staying at vacant homes to avoid being homeless.   He knows this was illegal to do but he contends he never stole from the homes."

"How is it possible that he stayed only at homes that were robbed?   Isn't that too much of a coincidence? "

"I agree…but I can prove he stayed at least one other home that was not burglarized. He said the first house he stayed at was at 1723 Stoney Point.   I personally went with a finger print specialist and checked for finger prints at this location."

"What did you find when you checked for finger prints at 1723 Stoney Point?"   Jill asked with anticipation.

"Mr. Johnson told us he was extremely careful to not touch anything at this house. We weren't sure we would find anything…but we did."

"And what did you find?"

"We found one perfect index finger print of Peter Johnson's in this house proving he was in the house even though the elderly couple that owned it had no idea someone had been in their house. She said nothing was missing and no burglary had been committed."

"Where did you find this finger print?"

"It was on the underside of the toilet seat. It was probably still there after this amount of time because only an elderly woman lived there and she probably did not ever raise the toilet seat."

"The Prosecution rests."

Chapter #37

In closing

"In closing," Jill strolled back and forth in front of the jury. "Peter Johnson admits that he trespassed in three houses without the owner's permission. He admits this was wrong to do. Through pure coincidence he became tangled in the middle of a burglary ring. Though he worked with one of the accused, there is no reason to believe that he was part of their gang yet alone the leader since two of the accused could not pick him out of a line up. We can also prove with finger prints that he was at each house plus an additional house that did not get robbed which helps to collaborate his trespass story. We can prove with DNA that he performed CPR on the victim Frank Crawford. Who does that?" she inquired looking at the nervous faces of the jurors. " Definitely not a murderer!"

"Peter Johnson has now served three months in jail and has been beaten up by other inmates numerous times while incarcerated." Jill sadly shook her head in sorrow for what Peter has gone through because of being in jail.

"All we have to prove today," Jill stated as she talked to the jury of twelve."Is that there were other people besides Peter Johnson that had the opportunity and motive to commit burglary and ultimately be responsible for the death of Frank Crawford."

"According to the statues of our law you must be *convinced* that Peter Johnson did willfully, and with premeditation, murder Frank Crawford without a shadow of a doubt in order to find him guilty of this offense. I think we have shown that other people, besides Mr. Johnson, had equal opportunity and/or motive to commit this crime." To make her point she paused and looked over at the table where Jenny Swenson, Roy Myers and Sam Lawsen were now seated. Then she returned her attention to the jury.

"You *must* find Peter Johnson innocent of premeditated murder and burglary. He should be released with time already served to pay for his trespass offenses." Jill closed with a deep sigh. Closings always drained her of every ounce of energy in her body. But she had given it her best.

The jury was sequestered to deliberate.

Chapter #38

Pam and Drake

The sun shone so bright in the sky. Its warmth seemed to soak all the way down to his bones. But it was time to get up from the park bench and get back to work.

It had been a year since the jury decided Peter was innocent of burglary and premeditated murder. A few months later Sam Lawsen was found guilty of manslaughter and burglary. Jenny Swenson was charged with burglary and Roy Myers was charged with burglary but got a reduced sentence in a plea bargain.

Peter Johnson was convicted with trespassing but due to the three months time served before the trial he was released that day. Jerry Posia allowed him to stay at his mother's house for a few months until he could get a job and get ahead. In time, he got a job managing a large apartment complex and spends his days painting, landscaping, mowing yards and cleaning out apartments after someone moves out. He was also given a very nice apartment to live in as part of his pay.

Within a few months Pam and Drake moved in with him and they were married with Drake as the ring bearer. Drake no longer called him "Peeta."   His new name for him was "Daddy."

Peter also helped remodel Ma's restaurant, by giving her his free labor, as his way to repay her for her kindness. She still 'finds' goodies to send home that would *'go to waste if he didn't take them.'*

His divorce is now final and he is glad to have that behind him. He regrets how he treated Betsy. He is no longer that type of man.

He and his wife Pam are now expecting a baby girl, due in six months. Ma is going to be the babies Godmother and Jerry Posia will be the babies Godfather.

Peter is so excited for his new life and for the new attitude he has. He is very grateful to everyone that stood by him.